Susannah stood. In a slow, deliberate motion, she bent and retrieved the sewing basket then turned toward him.

Her back stiffening, she fixed him with an icy glare. "Captain Sutton, I've come to learn that promises are as fragile as blown glass. George promised to return from Texas. He didn't. The canal builders promised the canal would bring prosperity. It hasn't. And now you have come with your plans for a railroad that will, in all probability, put my inn out of business."

Her tone had softened, but the bitterness remained. "Where was God's help and mercy when George's father died suddenly a month after George left for the army? Where was God when George fell in Texas or the floods washed out the canal for the better part of a year? No, Captain, I don't put much stock in promises."

Thad's heart ached as he watched her walk back into the inn. He longed to help her understand that only faith in God brings peace in times of trouble. But how could he, when his own doing had contributed to at least a portion of her problems?

C0-AKC-183

RAMONA K. CECIL is a wife, mother, grandmother, freelance poet, and award-winning inspirational romance writer. Now empty nesters, she and her husband make their home in Indiana. A member of American Christian Fiction Writers and American Christian Fiction Writers Indiana Chapter, her work has won awards in a number of inspirational writing contests. Over eighty of her inspirational verses have been published on a wide array of items for the Christian gift market. She enjoys a speaking ministry, sharing her journey to publication while encouraging aspiring writers. When not writing, her hobbies include reading, gardening, and visiting places of historical interest.

Books by Ramona K. Cecil

HEARTSONG PRESENTS
HP792—Sweet Forever

Don't miss out on any of our super romances. Write to us at the following address for information on our newest releases and club information.

Heartsong Presents Readers' Service
PO Box 721
Uhrichsville, OH 44683

Or visit www.heartsongpresents.com

Everlasting Promise

Ramona K. Cecil

Heartsong Presents

Special thanks to: The Canal Society of Indiana and historians Bob and Carolyn Schmidt; Historic Metamora and historian Paul Baudendistel; Cambridge City Library, Cambridge City, Indiana, and historian Patty Hersberger; Kim Sawyer for her invaluable critique work; and my husband, Jim, and daughters, Jennifer and Kelly, whose love, encouragement, and support for what I do never falters.

A note from the Author:
I love to hear from my readers! You may correspond with me by writing:

Ramona K. Cecil
Author Relations
PO Box 721
Uhrichsville, OH 44683

ISBN 978-1-60260-070-6

EVERLASTING PROMISE

Copyright © 2008 by Ramona K. Cecil. All rights reserved. Except for use in any review, the reproduction or utilization of this work in whole or in part in any form by any electronic, mechanical, or other means, now known or hereafter invented, is forbidden without the permission of Heartsong Presents, an imprint of Barbour Publishing, Inc., PO Box 721, Uhrichsville, Ohio 44683.

All scripture quotations are taken from the King James Version of the Bible.

All of the characters and events in this book are fictitious. Any resemblance to actual persons, living or dead, or to actual events is purely coincidental.

Our mission is to publish and distribute inspirational products offering exceptional value and biblical encouragement to the masses.

PRINTED IN THE U.S.A.

one

The sharp, clear notes of a bugle yanked Susannah Killion's attention from the pot of beans. She turned from the stove to the inn's kitchen window. A quick glance confirmed the unexpected announcement.

A canal boat, its hull emblazoned with a gold eagle in full wingspread, neared the canal basin wharf.

The Flying Eagle? Hadn't Garrett Heywood said that his boat would be undergoing repairs in Cincinnati and wouldn't be making the trip to Promise this week?

The happy chatter of the boat passengers wafted up from the canal basin a few yards from the inn's back door.

Susannah smoothed back an errant strand of hair straggling across her forehead and tucked it behind her ear. A coach was due off the National Road in less than an hour, and she hadn't planned nearly enough supper to accommodate guests from both the stagecoach and the canal boat.

The prayer for strength budding in her breast withered. Let Naomi pray. Susannah had stopped expecting answers to her prayers long ago.

Watching the line of people making their way toward the inn, she blew out a resigned sigh. She had neither the time nor the energy for futile prayers or self-pity.

"Susannah, the beans!" The alarm in her mother-in-law's voice whirled her around.

A *hiss* sent Susannah bounding to the stove. She grabbed a towel from a wall hook and snatched the hot lid off the

5

cast-iron pot, letting it fall to the stovetop with a clatter.

The acrid smell of burned beans filled the inn's little kitchen.

Susannah's heart drooped. *Perfect!* In another moment, hungry guests would be filing into the building, and the unappealing aroma would definitely not enhance their first impressions of the Killion House Inn.

A mixture of sympathy and dismay played across Naomi Killion's face before she turned to greet the packet passengers at the inn's side door.

Susannah transferred the salvageable portion of beans and ham to another pot, almost wishing she still believed in prayer. But prayer wouldn't feed her guests. A heaping bowl of mashed potatoes and a platter of fried ham would. Mentally brushing aside the urge to reach out for divine assistance, she headed for the pantry. Hadn't the past four years taught her to depend on no one but herself?

❧

Thad Sutton's stomach knotted as he disembarked from Captain Heywood's canal packet. Gripped by trepidation, he gazed at the rear of the three-story brick building before him. He wondered how the conflicting feelings of relief and dread could, at once, dwell together in a man's breast.

The journey from Cincinnati had taxed his patience, the trip alternating between mind-numbing boredom and physical exhaustion. Each of the half dozen times they ran aground, the captain had commandeered him, along with the other able-bodied male passengers, to help pole the boat into a floatable depth of water—twice during a chilly April shower. What little sleep he had acquired the past couple nights aboard Captain Heywood's packet had been fitful, disturbed incessantly by a group of young rowdies on their way to the California goldfields.

The young ruffians, their minds filled with dreams of riches and their bellies filled with whiskey, had kept all aboard awake with riotous conversation, singing, and discharging of their firearms—two rounds of which had barely missed Thad's bunk last night.

With each passing hour on the canal boat, Thad came to agree with his father's assessment—the Whitewater Canal was an ill-begotten folly, best replaced by a railroad with all possible expedience. With that precise goal in mind, his father had convinced his fellow board members of the Union Railway Company to hire Thad as engineer and surveyor.

The corner of Thad's mouth tugged into a sardonic grin. Nothing he'd done before had bought him an iota of respect in his father's eyes. Not his two years of service as captain of a U.S. Army regiment in Texas or his decorations for valor at the Battle of Buena Vista. But at the moment of his appointment to this post, he had seen the esteem he'd longed to earn shining in his father's eyes. Because he had found favor with Josiah Sutton's beloved Union Railway Company, Thad had at last basked in the admiration of his usually cool and distant parent.

However, he realized his father's rare display of approval came with a caveat. Thad was expected to deliver a short, direct, and cost-effective railroad route from Cincinnati to Indianapolis.

He'd pleased the board by quickly accomplishing the work up to forty miles southwestward of Indianapolis. And now, having accumulated the mathematical calculations needed from the Cincinnati end of the project, he was ready to do the work on this stretch along the Whitewater Canal. Situated in the approximate center of the forty-mile area he'd be surveying, the town of Promise, Indiana, seemed the ideal base from which to work. It also gave him an opportunity to repair an oversight in his duty to the widow of one of his fallen Army subordinates.

Though glad to have ended the tedious trip from Cincinnati, he did not especially relish the meeting awaiting him within the walls of this unpretentious inn. He pressed his fingers against his navy blue broadcloth coat. The crinkle of paper he felt against his chest reminded him—as if he needed any reminding—that he'd been derelict in his duty four years ago. Somehow, instead of sending George Killion's last letter on to his widow, Susannah, Thad recently discovered he'd accidentally filed it away among letters he'd received from his own family during the war. No, he did not look forward to admitting his error to George Killion's widow.

Susannah Killion. He would have no trouble recognizing the woman. Her pleasant, comely features seemed burned into his brain. He could close his eyes and see her smiling at him from the daguerreotype George had placed in his keeping.

What reaction was he to expect from her in response to his grievous negligence? Tears? Anger? He'd marched unflinchingly into battle dozens of times on the dusty Texas plains. And right now, he would much prefer facing a full regiment of Santa Anna's best rather than the Widow Killion.

Stepping from the boat, Thad's stomach growled, and the knot in his gut cinched tighter. The food aboard the *Flying Eagle* had been a bit too heavy on the grease for his taste. Hopefully, Susannah Killion's table offered better fare.

That hope withered when a slight, middle-aged woman ushered him, along with the other travelers, into the Killion House Inn. The unappetizing smell of burned beans assaulted his nostrils and caused his spirit to groan with his stomach.

At the massive desk in the lobby, he signed in and accepted the little brass room key from the woman who'd introduced herself as Naomi Killion. If George Killion's mother recognized his name, she showed no sign of it, turning to focus on the couple behind him who were demanding a room with an easterly view.

Thad started up the staircase, lugging his carpetbag and case of surveyor's instruments. He would introduce himself formally to George's mother later. Glancing down at the lobby, he hitched up his courage for his impending meeting with the man's widow.

≈

After putting a large pot of potatoes on to boil and slicing down a quarter of a smoked ham, Susannah crossed the kitchen and headed to the hallway linen closet. By now, Naomi would have all the passengers from the packet signed in and shown to their rooms.

She snatched the feather duster from the closet's top shelf. While she waited for the potatoes to cook, she'd give the lobby a quick go-over. As she scanned the walnut-paneled sitting area, she couldn't help the pride welling up inside her. No other inn within fifty miles had as elegant a lobby. Her late father-in-law had gone into debt to make it so.

She crossed the rose-patterned carpet, maneuvering between the horsehair sofa and green velvet settee. At the fireplace, she swiped the duster across the stone mantel and repositioned one of the gold silk wing chairs flanking the hearth.

After flicking the feather duster over the two marble-topped tables on either side of the sofa, she breathed a contented sigh. Despite the hard work and demanding life, Susannah loved this inn with all her heart. And now, with the canal navigable again, the inn was actually beginning to prosper. For three months in a row, she'd been able to put a little extra money aside.

Though harried, Susannah realized this was one of the better days. Most of the rooms would be filled tonight. The canal had been operational again for several months, and spring had brought an increase in stagecoach travelers. Even the worrisome rumors of a railroad that would threaten the existence of the entire town of Promise, as well as the Killion House Inn, seemed to have subsided.

She redeposited the duster in the closet and started for the stairs. Thankfully, Naomi had put Georgiana down for a nap a half hour ago. But Susannah decided she'd best check on her four-year-old before returning to the kitchen.

"Mrs. Killion?"

Susannah paused at the bottom of the staircase and turned to discover who possessed the quiet male voice.

"Mrs. George Killion?" With a few quick strides, a man closed the distance between the sitting area and stairway. There was nothing alarming in the elegant dress or quiet demeanor of the handsome young gentleman, yet something about him made Susannah's heart quake.

"Yes." Susannah turned to face the traveler. He stood about six feet in height, she guessed. His brown hair curled slightly over his ears. He had a strong-looking face with a square jaw that tapered to a cleft chin. The only remarkable feature about him was the intense look in his gray eyes.

"I'm sorry, sir. I thought my mother-in-law had registered all the new guests." Susannah took a step toward the main desk.

His hurried words stopped her. "I have acquired my room. Thank you, ma'am." He dipped a low bow. "Thaddeus Sutton—Captain Thaddeus Sutton—at your service, Mrs. Killion. If I may beg a moment of your time?"

Captain Sutton. . . Susannah's mind raced, trying to think why that name sounded familiar.

The man drew a yellowed envelope from a pocket inside his coat. "I'm afraid I've been tardy in delivering this missive."

As Susannah reached for the proffered letter, his next words sent her blood sluicing to her toes.

"It's from your husband, George."

Susannah's legs went weak, and she swayed with the room that seemed to swirl around her. A swarm of questions crowded her stunned mind as she slumped against the stranger who reached out strong arms to support her.

two

"It was a girl." Thad voiced his thoughts as his gaze followed the towheaded moppet scampering past him through the inn's dining room doorway.

"I beg your pardon?" Susannah Killion placed a bowl of mashed potatoes in the center of the long table and glanced up at him. Her placid expression suggested she'd sufficiently recovered from the shock he caused her an hour earlier when he handed her George's letter.

Once again, remorse smote Thad's heart at the memory of her delicate features blanching paper-white. He hadn't once thought that receiving such a letter might disturb her. Expecting her to be angry that he had not sent the letter to her years earlier, he never considered she might misconstrue its existence, thinking George had not died in Buena Vista after all. Shifting his gaze to the child sitting on the dining room floor, playing with her doll and munching on a biscuit, he wished with all his heart that were true.

He nodded toward Susannah Killion's little girl. "The child. I remember how George crowed for days after he received your letter telling him he was to be a father. It was the only thing that brought him consolation, learning at the same time about the death of his father."

"Did you know my husband well, Captain Sutton? He always spoke highly of you in his letters." She didn't look at him as she transferred a platter of ham to the table from a buffet against the south wall. He noticed a subtle stiffening of her demeanor, as if she were steeling herself against the painful subject.

"Yes—well, I suppose as well as any captain can know a

11

sergeant under his command." Thad marveled at her disciplined composure. He'd witnessed the same starch in her earlier when he handed her George's letter. For a moment, he'd feared she might faint dead away. Instead, his admiration for Susannah Killion had grown as he watched her battle her emotions while he explained that George had written the missive just prior to his death.

Thad moved toward the end of the table, hoping to change the subject. The conversation had taken a turn down a road he didn't care to travel. "Should I be seated, or do you have a seating order?"

"First come, first served." Her well-shaped lips lifted in the first true smile she'd given him. It sent warmth radiating through him, causing him to hope for many more of Susannah Killion's smiles.

As if mesmerized, his gaze followed her graceful movements around the long dining table. He'd always thought her picture attractive, but he now realized it was but a poor representation of the real woman. With a more than pleasing figure, hair the color of clover honey, and green eyes flecked with amber, Susannah Killion was heart-joltingly beautiful.

"Will you be returning to Cincinnati then, Captain Sutton?"

Several other patrons had filed into the dining room. Thad gripped the back of a chair near the end of the table and awaited the seating of the ladies. "No. Actually, I plan to use Killion House Inn as my residence for the next several months. In civilian life, I'm an engineer and surveyor and have come to do work along this stretch of the canal."

He'd taken a quick jaunt along the canal towpath and had made some preliminary notes. From what he had seen, the towpath seemed solid. Beyond that, he estimated it would be a challenge to find land solid enough on the marshy landscape to support tracks.

Surprise lit her hazel-green eyes and this time her smile lingered on him for a long, sweet moment. "Then we shall be glad to have you, Captain Sutton. Perhaps with your expertise, you can figure a way to keep floods from plaguing our canal."

Thad opened his mouth to correct her misunderstanding. But before he could, she hurried from the dining room just as a minister in the group pronounced a blessing over the supper.

❧

Susannah opened the top drawer of her cherrywood dresser to retrieve one of her Sunday-best embroidered handkerchiefs. Her gaze drifted to the envelope she'd tucked in the drawer's lower right-hand corner. It had been over a week since Captain Sutton handed her George's last letter, but she hadn't yet found the courage to open it.

She allowed her fingertips to glide across the yellowed paper. George's left-slanted handwriting brought a smile to her lips and a lump to her throat. He'd been left-handed all his life, to the consternation of every teacher who'd tried to set him right.

She remembered the autumn when they were eight years old and Mr. Greathouse first came to teach. George's poor little left hand had stayed swollen and red from constant raps of the new teacher's rod. Susannah had felt every whack dealt to her playmate's hand. Once, she'd tried to warn George to move his chalk to his right hand before the teacher noticed. They both were caught, spanked, and made to stand in opposite corners of the schoolhouse. From that day on, they'd been nearly inseparable.

The jumble of uncomfortable feelings that always accompanied thoughts of her late husband balled up in Susannah's chest. Their last day together had been filled with angry words. Sometimes at night, when she closed her eyes, she could still see George standing on the deck of the retreating canal boat, a gentle breeze ruffling the tangle of blond curls framing his boyish face. Susannah remembered how she'd stood on the bank watching him wave until the boat became a speck in the distance and she could no longer see the red bandanna tied about his neck. Because of her anger at his leaving, she'd refused to wave back.

It was the last time she saw him. Seven months later, he died at the Battle of Buena Vista.

She scrunched her eyes tight against the tears stinging the backs of her eyelids and tried to conjure up George's likeness. Fear gripped her when a clear picture of him would not develop. Instead, another visage shoved its way before her mind's eye.

Captain Sutton.

He had no right to intrude—to replace George's image with his own.

Her conscience pricked at her uncharitable thoughts of George's former commanding officer. In every one of his letters, George had nothing but the highest praise for Captain Sutton.

She picked up the envelope. Captain Sutton had cared enough to deliver George's last letter in person, albeit four years late. And he was here to work on the canal—the canal that brought patrons to the inn.

She turned the letter over and slipped a thumbnail beneath an edge near the sealing wax. Her hand froze. She couldn't bring herself to read the last words George had written to her. Somehow, to read this letter was to close the door on their marriage forever. She wasn't ready to do that. Maybe tomorrow. Maybe never. Susannah dropped the letter into the drawer and pushed it shut.

"Mamma, look what Tad taught me."

Wiping tears from her face, Susannah forced a smile as she turned at her daughter's excited voice.

"See?" Georgiana pulled herself up to her full height, stiffened, flattened her hand, and brought the edge of her index finger to her brow. "Tad taught me to salute."

Susannah couldn't help a tiny smile. "That's a fine salute, Georgiana, but girls don't join the Army, so I don't think saluting is something you'll need to know how to do."

Immediately smitten with Captain Sutton, Georgiana had spent the week since his arrival following him around the inn like a puppy. He, in turn, seemed to delight in her attention, often surprising her with penny candy from the general store when he returned from his daily forays along the canal.

Susannah appreciated the kindness Thaddeus Sutton showed her daughter. But she worried that Georgiana's attachment to the man might cause the child grief when he concluded his business here.

She bent to redo her daughter's crookedly buttoned dress. "You should really call him Captain Sutton instead of his given name. It's more respectful, don't you think?"

"But he told me to call him Tad," Georgiana argued as Susannah covered her daughter's blond curls with a little yellow bonnet and fashioned its ribbons into a bow beneath the child's chin.

"Captain Sutton's given name is Thad, not Tad. We need to work on your *th* sound."

As they descended the stairs, Susannah wrestled with her own confused feelings about Thaddeus Sutton while Georgiana practiced the correct pronunciation of his name.

"Th–Th–Thad. Th–Th–Thad. Tad!" Georgiana squealed with delight. Pulling away from Susannah's grasp, she scurried down the last few steps into the lobby. Susannah hurried to catch up with her daughter and felt her heart quicken. It was a response she'd come to expect whenever in the company of the handsome surveyor.

Clutching his dark beaver hat by the brim, Thaddeus Sutton swept a deep bow. "Would you lovely ladies do me the honor of allowing me to escort you to worship services?"

"Pease, Mamma, peaaase!" Georgiana bounced up and down in her yellow calico dress like a daffodil in a stiff spring breeze.

"That's very gracious of you, Captain, but. . ." Susannah

grappled for a reason to decline his offer. The effect the man had on Susannah unsettled her, and she'd found herself rebelling against it. She looked down at her silk skirt, smoothing an imaginary wrinkle from its pewter-colored folds. "Naomi's not quite ready yet, and I wouldn't want to keep you—"

"I'm here." Naomi bustled into the lobby, her slight figure swathed in black bombazine. "How gallant of you, Captain Sutton. We would be more than pleased to have your company, wouldn't we, Susannah?"

Outnumbered, Susannah surrendered. "Yes, thank you, Captain."

Taking his proffered right arm while Naomi accepted his left, Susannah scolded her unruly heart, which bounced and giggled along with Georgiana.

As they walked to the carriage house, he turned a devastating smile toward Susannah and she caught a faint wisp of bay rum and the clean smell of shaving soap. "Although it is a fine day and the church is only a few blocks away, I took the liberty of asking young Ruben to hitch that fine black gelding of yours to the phaeton. I hope you don't mind."

Her return smile came as easily to Susannah's lips as her honest answer. "Not at all, Captain Sutton." Under other circumstances, she might have thought the action impertinent. But instead, she felt both appreciation and relief for having a responsibility, however small, lifted from her shoulders.

As they neared the carriage house where her sixteen-year-old nephew, Ruben, waited with the horse and buggy, Thad again inclined his head toward her. "I was hoping after church I might prevail upon you to give me a proper tour of the town. I've seen little of it beyond the shops and houses that border the canal."

Thad paused to press several coins into Ruben's palm, winning Susannah's admiration with the show of kindness to her young kin. The captain helped Naomi into the back of the two-seat phaeton. Then he swung a giggling Georgiana in a wide arc before depositing her on the black leather seat beside her grandmother.

When he turned his full attention to Susannah, his twinkling gray eyes sent her heart into a canter. "Well, Mrs. Killion, will you show me Promise?" His strong hands grasped her waist, lifting her easily to the front seat.

During the preceding interlude, Susannah had tried and failed to think of a graceful way to decline his request. So the words that popped from her mouth surprised her. "Yes, of course." She wished her voice didn't sound so breathless.

As he settled beside her and took the reins, she found herself looking forward to the sightseeing excursion, and she turned a good-natured grin toward him. "Although your business is to improve the Whitewater Canal, you should know there is more to Promise than our glorious ditch."

He gave her a bemused look. "Forgive me, but I'm afraid you've misunderstood my work here. I have not come to improve the canal itself, but to survey for a railroad that would replace it."

three

Susannah reached into her pocket for another handful of hard, dry seed peas. Bending over the furrow Ruben had earlier gouged into the newly plowed and harrowed garden plot behind the inn, she dropped the seeds onto the earth with such force they bounced. Rising, she drew back her shoulders and stretched her spine. She closed her eyes, lifted her face, and allowed the April sun to bathe it in warmth. Perhaps the soothing rays would help calm her troubled mind.

Since Thaddeus Sutton's jarring revelation yesterday, she hadn't enjoyed a moment of peace. A battle raged inside her. Anger and fear warred for the upper hand. She had no doubt that anger would win out, for she could not abide the fear.

Another emotion clung to her heart like a dank mist. Disappointment.

The handsome surveyor with his gallant ways and winning smile had stridden into her heart, awakening feelings she thought she'd never experience again. Then, in a matter-of-fact tone, he'd uttered the devastating statement that unleashed the conflict still clashing inside her.

Susannah had enjoyed the cordiality that marked their acquaintance, promising a burgeoning friendship. It still pained her to discover they were destined to be adversaries.

And how could she explain to Georgiana that her beloved "Tad," who gave her penny candy and piggyback rides, represented the industry that would snatch away their home and livelihood?

Susannah pressed her fingers to her throbbing temples.

"Are you pwaying, Mamma?"

At Georgiana's voice, Susannah's eyes flew open. "No, honey,

Mamma just has a little headache." She managed a tiny smile as guilt rippled through her. It had been a long time since she'd made a conscious effort to pray—even in church.

"Gwamma closes her eyes when she pways."

"Prays, Georgiana. You can pronounce your *r*'s if you try. I've heard you do it."

"Well, she does when she prr–ays."

"Good girl. See, I knew you could do it." Susannah hoped to steer her daughter toward a less troublesome topic.

"Look, Mamma, I planted lots of peas." Georgiana beamed as she pointed to the crooked trail of seeds she'd scattered along the furrow ahead of them. "Tad said he likes peas and we should plant a bunch."

"Georgiana. . ." Susannah grappled for the right words as she bent to pick up the hoe from between two rows of planted seeds. "Georgiana, it is good that you want to please our guests," she said as she began raking dirt over the peas then gently tamping it down with the flat of the hoe blade. "That means you are a good innkeeper. But as I've told you before, you must not become too attached to any of the guests because they are not here to stay."

"Tad is not a guest. He is my friend. He's going to let me look through his spyglass. He pwomised—prr–omised!" Scowling, Georgiana firmly planted dirty fists on her little hips.

Susannah ignored her daughter's indignant tone and stance. "Very good, Georgiana. See, you can pronounce your *r*'s." Then, feeling her smile fade, she hunched down next to her child. She brushed away a smudge of soil from the apple of Georgiana's soft, pink cheek. "Georgiana, I'd rather you didn't bother Captain Sutton or his surveying instruments."

Georgiana, her face sullen, never answered as Susannah poked a stick into the soft earth to mark the end of the planted row.

"Four rows should be plenty." Hefting the hoe in her left

hand, Susannah took Georgiana's hand in her right and led her daughter back to the inn. Knowing the child's attention flitted from one thing to another like the robins hopping about the garden plot, she figured if she dropped the subject of Thad Sutton, Georgiana would, too.

But the moment they stepped into the kitchen, she learned she was wrong.

Georgiana raced to her grandmother, who stood at the washstand. "Grr–amma, me and Mamma planted lots of peas 'cause Tad likes 'em. Won't he be happy?"

Drying her hands on a towel, Naomi Killion turned and gave her granddaughter a fond smile. "I should think Captain Sutton will be very pleased, indeed."

"I planted almost as many seeds as Mamma did, but she had to stop. Not to pw–prr–ay, but 'cause her head hurts," Georgiana told her grandmother as Naomi wet a cloth in a pan of water and began washing dirt from the child's hands.

Naomi sent Susannah a quick glance that promised a sermon the moment they were alone then turned back to Georgiana. "Now, I think it is time for you and Dolly to have tea in the lobby, don't you? You know how particular Dolly is about her tea time."

Georgiana gave a somber nod and headed toward the doorway that led to the lobby. "Dolly gets very cwoss when she misses her tea."

Susannah didn't look forward to time alone with her mother-in-law. Though she loved Naomi as if she were her own blood, their relationship had been strained for the past several months. An uncomfortable stiffness had replaced the easiness with which they'd shared their lives since they became mother and daughter. And Susannah knew she bore a large portion of blame for the change.

Naomi seemed to have sensed the erosion of Susannah's faith. Susannah knew her mother-in-law couldn't understand why the tragedies of the past several years had diluted her faith when they'd strengthened Naomi's.

"A little prayer from time to time would not go amiss, daughter," Naomi said quietly as she passed Susannah, carrying the pan of dirty water toward the back door.

The faint hint of reproach in her mother-in-law's voice sent a prickle of irritation up Susannah's back. "You pray enough for all of us, Naomi."

Naomi opened the back door and pitched the water outside. "I'm concerned that you are pulling away from the Lord," she said as she shut the door and headed back to the washstand with the empty pan. "Even Georgiana has begun to notice. It's not a good example for the child." She poured hot water into the pan from a kettle on the stove then tempered it with cold water from a bucket beside the washstand.

"And I'm concerned that you continue to encourage Georgiana's friendship with that. . .that man!" Susannah reached up and snatched a large crockery bowl from the shelf beside the stove. She plunked it down onto the table so hard she wondered that it hadn't cracked.

"Captain Sutton? Why, that young man is pure Christian kindness. I can see why George spoke so well of him." Naomi gave a little chuckle that sent another trail of annoyance rasping along Susannah's spine.

Susannah pointed toward the window that framed the canal basin. "At this very moment, that man is out designing a railroad route that would ruin our inn—this inn Papa Emil and George left to our keeping!"

"Captain Sutton is simply doing the job he was sent here to do, nothing more. What happens as a result of his work is in God's hands." With infuriating calmness, Naomi went back to washing the stack of stoneware dishes and cups.

The quiet clinking of dishes filled the uneasy silence between the two women.

Susannah breathed a deep sigh and headed for the lobby to check on Georgiana. She didn't like quarreling with Naomi, but sometimes Susannah felt as if she was the only one willing to fight for their home.

And fight she would, even if her enemy was the charming Captain Sutton.

&

At the rumbling sound of a farm wagon passing on the National Road, Thad paused in recording the measurements he'd just taken. Transferring the pencil and record book to one hand, he waved and hailed a friendly greeting across the canal to the farmer.

When the man glanced toward him, his smile turned to a dark glower. The farmer's hand, which he'd raised momentarily in return salutation, shot back down to grasp the reins draped across the draft horse's rump.

The farmer turned his attention back to the road, and an uncomfortable feeling twisted through Thad's chest. He lifted the transit from the tripod and placed it in its leather case. Then, for a long moment, he stood watching the farmer's slump-shouldered back, now obscured by the road dust kicked up by the wagon wheels.

It seemed increasingly clear to Thad that the majority of Promise had little use for him or his business.

While most communities welcomed the prospect of a railroad, Promise was not among them. Many here had helped to build the Whitewater Canal. For years they'd fought for it, enduring floods that washed out locks and culverts. Thad was aware that some residents had even donated money to the Whitewater Canal Company to fund repairs on the waterway when the state refused to throw good money after bad.

The citizens of Promise had poured both emotional and financial capital into the sorry ditch. They seemed to look upon it as a long-ill kinsman, only now gaining a measure of vigor. Thad knew they viewed him as someone who'd come to deal the canal a deathblow just as it rose from its sickbed.

In truth, he understood why the people of Promise held him

in distain. But the reality was that a railroad would be coming. Maybe not next year, or even in five years, but eventually one *would* come. He might as well be the one to chart its path. Besides, his father had left little doubt that failure to do so was not an option.

Only the regard of one person shook his resolve.

Susannah Killion.

The look in her eyes yesterday, when he'd explained his business here, still haunted him. His insides had twisted painfully when the soft lines of her sweet face hardened in contempt. But it was the stark fear he'd seen flicker in her green eyes that had kept him awake last night.

He wished he could assure her that the Union Railway Company would situate a passenger depot in Promise, but he knew that possibility was remote.

Thad blew out a long breath as he lashed the tripod to the back of Chieftain, the roan stallion he'd purchased for his longer treks along the canal. He might as well accept the fact that he'd killed any possibility of winning the favor of the lovely Susannah Killion.

As he rode toward Promise, he realized the only residents who ever offered him a greeting or ready smile were Naomi Killion and her granddaughter, Georgiana.

Thoughts of the blond cherub lifted his spirits along with the corners of his mouth. The child had quickly entangled her chubby fingers in his heartstrings. What joy to watch her little face beam as he handed her a piece of penny candy, a spinning top, or a length of colored ribbon for her hair.

As he neared the inn's back door, Susannah Killion emerged from the building, holding a basket against her trim waist.

The sight set his heart prancing. Dismounting, Thad smiled and dipped a quick bow. "Mrs. Killion."

"Captain Sutton." With an unsmiling but pleasant voice, she murmured the quiet acknowledgment and settled herself on the top step with the little basket beside her. She reached into the basket, lifted out a square cloth he recognized as a table napkin, and began working a needle around the edge of the material.

Trying to think of something to say, Thad looked behind the inn where he could see a dark brown patch of tilled ground. "Georgiana told me yesterday that the two of you were planning to plant peas this morning." He tethered Chieftain to a low branch of a large, old pin oak. Tender young leaves had begun emerging from the buds that tipped the tree's branches. When fully grown, the leaves would shade the entire east quadrant of the backyard.

While the horse munched on grass, Thad settled himself on the bench beneath the tree. He prayed that a congenial chat might help to restore the friendliness he and Susannah Killion seemed to have lost. "Fine day for making a garden. Extra warm for the middle of April."

"Yes, I suppose it is." A hint of a smile touched her lips, raising his hopes, but she didn't elaborate.

For several moments, Thad sat still, content to soak in the lovely picture of the late morning sun lacing golden threads through her honey-colored hair. The honking of a gaggle of geese near the canal basin punctuated the lengthening silence. As he contemplated what sufficiently intelligent comment he might offer in way of further conversation, she spoke first.

"I trust your work has been going well, Captain."

He started at her unexpected comment, feeling heat rise from his neck to his face. The subject of his work would not have been his choice of conversation, so he attempted to change it. "Yes—that is, on such a beautiful day, it's a blessing to have an opportunity to work outside." His gaze swept from the azure sky decorated with cotton clouds to the lush meadow separating the canal and a strip of woods. "My aunt Edith would have called this an extra glad day."

"Extra glad?" Now her pink, Cupid's bow lips stretched to a full smile, showing straight white teeth. Her smile elicited the same feeling in Thad as when the clouds parted, allowing the sunshine to pour over him.

"Yes, as in Psalm 118. 'This is the day which the Lord hath made; we will rejoice and be glad in it.'" Even to his own ears, he sounded as breathless as if he'd run a quarter-mile foot race.

She only nodded, and her smile faded as she returned her attention to the work in her lap.

Thad wondered at her change in demeanor but, determined to keep their conversation going, he allowed his gaze to travel from the fertile fields left of the canal basin to the bustling infant town on its right.

"Promise. This place must be peopled with folk full of faith in the divine Word."

Susannah didn't look up from her busy fingers continuing to deftly work the needle around the piece of cloth. "Some more, some less, I reckon."

"And in which camp do you consider yourself?" Thad regretted the question the moment it left his lips.

Her fingers stilled. She lifted her face, and he read her answer in the empty look in her hazel-green eyes. "Reckon I quit believin' in promises, divine or otherwise, when I got your letter four years ago informing me of George's death."

Sadness and guilt twined together around Thad's heart, cinching tight until he winced inwardly. "But you continue to attend worship services. . . ." He turned his gaze toward the town's little church. He could see the white steeple three blocks away. Like a resolute arm, it thrust the symbol of the cross from the midst of surrounding sycamores into the clear blue sky.

Her lips lifted in a wry grin. "That's mainly to pacify Naomi." She dropped her gaze to the work in her hands and started moving the needle in and out of the cloth again.

At her reply, Thad felt irritation skitter through him, setting a sharp edge to his voice. "George was Naomi's son, and she hasn't lost her faith."

Susannah stood. In a slow, deliberate motion, she bent and retrieved the sewing basket then turned toward him. Her back stiffening, she fixed him with an icy glare. "Captain Sutton, I've come to learn that promises are as fragile as blown glass. George promised to return from Texas. He didn't. The canal builders promised the canal would bring prosperity. It hasn't. And now you have come with your plans for a railroad that will, in all probability, put my inn out of business."

Her tone had softened, but the bitterness remained. "Where was God's help and mercy when George's father died suddenly a month after George left for the army? Where was God when George fell in Texas or the floods washed out the canal for the better part of a year? No, Captain, I don't put much stock in promises."

Thad's heart ached as he watched her walk back into the inn. He longed to help her understand that only faith in God brings peace in times of trouble. But how could he, when his own doing had contributed to at least a portion of her problems?

four

Pirouette.

Yes, that was the word—pirouette. Last fall, a woman traveling on the stagecoach to Indianapolis had shown Susannah a playbill from a ballet she'd attended in New York. The playbill depicted lady dancers in filmy pink dresses. They stood on tiptoe with their arms arced above their heads. The woman said they would actually twirl on their toes. She called it, "Doing a pirouette."

That's how Susannah felt each time she looked at Thad Sutton. Her heart did a pirouette.

From the back door of the inn, she gazed across the meadow at the surveyor striding through knee-high grass, his tripod resting on his shoulder.

Her heart spun like a ballerina.

Something in his purposeful gait and the strong, chiseled lines of the man took her breath away. A freshened breeze ruffled his wavy brown hair. His shirtsleeves, rolled above his elbows, revealed strong, tanned forearms. She caught faint snatches of a happy whistled tune wafting from his striding figure. Though too far away to see, Susannah could imagine a twinkle in his gray eyes.

Unable to make her heart dislike the man, she had grudgingly come to agree with Naomi's rationalization—Captain Sutton was just doing his job.

In no way did her decision alter her fear and dislike of the railroad or diminish her fervent hope that his work here would prove unsuccessful. Each morning she awoke with half her heart wishing he would leave and the other half fearing he might.

A tug at her skirt wrenched her attention from the troublesome Captain Sutton.

"I got a sack for the gweens, Mamma."

"Good, Georgiana. That's good," she answered absently, not bothering to correct her daughter's mispronounced word. Her gaze drifted back to the man walking toward them.

"Tad!" Georgiana caught sight of her hero and bounded toward Thad Sutton, trailing the yellow calico sack behind her like a pennant.

"Georgiana!" Susannah called after her.

The mother's admonishing tone ignored, she sprinted to catch up with her daughter, allowing the basket on her arm to bounce against her side.

"Well, Miss Georgiana! Where are you off to this fine day?" With a wide grin, Thad Sutton dropped his surveyor's tools to the ground and snatched up the giggling Georgiana, swinging her in a wide arc against the blue sky.

Georgiana's breathless answer tumbled out as he set her feet back on the ground. "Mamma and I are going to hunt mushwooms and gweens. See, here's my sack. It's for the gweens." She held up the calico sack.

"Well, that should hold a nice mess of greens." His broad smile swung from Georgiana to Susannah, setting her heart twirling on its toes again.

"May I look thwough your spyglass now, Tad? Will you go mushwoom hunting with us?"

"Georgiana, you shouldn't bother the captain." Susannah took Georgiana's hand and drew her to her side, causing her daughter's hopeful face to droop. "And you should not address Captain Sutton by his given name." Susannah's face heated as much from the twinkle in Thad Sutton's gray eyes as her daughter's lack of etiquette. "I apologize, Captain Sutton. I really have taught her better manners."

He shook his head at her apology. "Georgiana and I are friends, and friends should address one another by their first names." His gaze seemed to melt into hers. "I would like to consider us friends as well and would be honored if you'd address me as Thad. May I be so bold as to call you Susannah?"

"Well, I. . ." The plea in his eyes dried up her intended refusal of his suggestion. "Certainly, Cap—Thad."

"May I? May I look thwough your spyglass?" Georgiana, her wilted expression revived, tugged at his pant leg.

"Sure," he said with a chuckle, "if it's all right with your mamma."

At Susannah's nod, he knelt beside Georgiana and un-latched the leather case. He took out what looked like a telescope mounted on a short tripod above a compass.

Susannah gave a little gasp when Thad allowed Georgiana to grasp the telescope. "Be very careful, Georgiana."

Thad shot her a grin as Georgiana leaned an eye against the telescope lens. "Nothing to be concerned about, Susannah. Old William J. Young made these things nearly indestructible."

"Ooh, the twees look so close!" Georgiana giggled as she alternately peered through the telescope at the little woods behind the inn then looked without the benefit of its magnification. She turned wide eyes toward Thad. "I saw a birdie in its nest!"

He chuckled, and Susannah wondered why she hadn't noticed before how the right corner of his mouth dimpled when he smiled.

"Now," he told Georgiana as he nestled the transit back into its case, "we'd better not use up any more of your mamma's morning."

"Will you. . . ," Georgiana heaved a sigh laden with frus-tration. "Will you come mushwoom hunting with us?"

"That sounds like great fun. I haven't gone mushroom hunt-ing since I was a boy." His gray gaze lingered on Susannah's, causing her heart to flutter and her face to grow warm. "But we'd need to ask your mamma if I might accompany your hunt."

Georgiana grabbed a fistful of Susannah's skirt and tugged. "Peaase? Peaase, Mamma, may Tad come?"

"Yes, of course, if we are not keeping you from your work—Thad." Susannah stumbled over his name and scolded herself for feeling as giddy as Georgiana about the prospect of Thad Sutton's company.

"Work can wait. It's not every day I get an invitation to a mushroom hunt." He bent and retrieved the tripod poles and transit case. "If you ladies will indulge me for a few moments while I return my instruments to my room, I'll rejoin you directly."

While she and Georgiana waited beneath the oak tree, Susannah struggled with her conflicting feelings about Thad joining them. The man was too bothersome by half! She should have simply refused him. Surely she could have thought of something. But that would have meant disappointing Georgiana.

She glanced at her daughter, who was bouncing up and down while gleefully mispronouncing Captain Sutton's name. Susannah followed Georgiana's adoring gaze. Watching Thad emerge from the inn's back door, she knew it hadn't been the prospect of a whiny child that had caused her to agree to his company.

Striding toward them, he clapped his outstretched hands toward her daughter. "How about a piggyback ride, Georgiana?" At the child's enthusiastic nod, he laughed and swung her up to his shoulders.

They waded their way through the tall grass toward the woods, and Susannah couldn't help thinking what a perfect picture of domestic contentment the three of them must make. At the troubling thought, she accelerated her pace, marching ahead of Georgiana and the captain.

The refreshing coolness of the forest greeted her as she pushed aside the branches of an elderberry bush and stepped beneath the canopy of young leaves. The woodsy scents of bark, moss, decaying leaves, and wildflowers tickled her nose.

"Mamma, don't go so fast! Wait for me and Tad." Rustling leaves and snapping twigs accompanied Georgiana's complaint.

Susannah glanced over her shoulder at her daughter. Now back on the ground, Georgiana ran toward her, ahead of Captain Sutton.

"Tad and I already got some dandelion gweens." Georgiana held open her yellow sack.

"Greens, Georgiana. Remember your *r*'s."

Joining them, Thad tousled Georgiana's curls. "I hope we didn't delay you, Susannah, but we found a nice patch of dandelions near a big sycamore."

"No—no, not at all." Susannah busied herself picking an elderberry leaf from Georgiana's hair. It seemed odd to hear Captain Sutton address her by her given name. What was more disconcerting—she realized she liked it.

"I see some gwe–grr–eens!" Georgiana bounded toward a sun-dappled clearing.

"Don't go far," Susannah cautioned. "Don't step in mud puddles, and watch out for snakes."

"You're doing a wonderful job with her." Thad's voice pulled Susannah's attention from Georgiana, who crouched a few feet away, picking dandelion greens. "The inn and raising a daughter—I don't know how you do it all. As my aunt Edith would say, 'You're a caution and a wonder.'"

Susannah warmed beneath his praise. Keeping her gaze fixed on the forest floor, she maneuvered around several puddles. Recent rains had made the woods marshy, but Susannah knew the dampness along with the warm spring sun promised a bounty of mushrooms.

"I'm not sure I could do it without Naomi." Casting a quick, reassuring glance at Georgiana, Susannah headed toward a decaying elm stump.

Thad chuckled. "Yes, she's a caution and a wonder, too. I think Naomi and Aunt Edith would get on quite well."

"You must be very close to your aunt Edith." Susannah had wondered at his several references to his relative.

"Yes. After my mother died when I was about Georgiana's age, my father left me with his sister, Edith, and her husband while he pursued various business ventures. She and my uncle Joe nearly raised me in Vernon, down in Jennings County."

"You are not close to your father, then?" Susannah watched his face cloud and wished she had not voiced her thought.

"No." His terse reply increased her regret.

He focused his attention on the far side of a decaying tree stump, and his tone brightened. "Ah, here is what we are looking for," he announced, seeming as happy to change the subject as to find the mushrooms.

He knelt and brushed black humus from the rotting wood, revealing a large cluster of honeycomb mushrooms. Taking a small knife from his pocket, Thad sliced through the spongy beige stems and handed the grayish-brown fungus spears to Susannah.

"I can see you've had experience in mushroom hunting, Captain Sutton." Susannah chuckled as she carefully arranged the delicate mushrooms in her linen-lined basket.

"Thad, remember?" A hurt look flickered in his eyes for an instant before his smile vanquished it. "As a boy, I spent many a spring day hunting mushrooms with Uncle Joe in the woods along the Muscatatuck River." His gaze panned the immediate area. "You seem very familiar with this little wood. Were you raised in Promise?"

"No, George and I were both raised in Hamilton County."

They made their way toward Georgiana, who had abandoned her greens hunting to study a black and yellow butterfly flitting about a patch of bluebells a few yards away.

"Do you still have family there?" Thad took Susannah's hand and helped her over a fallen tree.

"Only my older brother, Frank, and his family."

"Ruben's father?"

Susannah's voice lowered. "Yes." Frank's displeasure with her for taking Ruben in and allowing him to work for her rather than sending him back home still chaffed. Though Thad seemed genuinely interested in her family history, Susannah did not feel comfortable divulging the rift that decision had caused between her and her brother.

"And your parents, do they still live there?"

"No, they died of cholera when I was twelve." A painful stab near Susannah's heart accompanied the memory of that awful summer day when she lost her parents. She remembered how she'd fought to enter the quarantined cabin when she learned of their deaths. And how Ephraim, her doctor brother-in-law, would not allow her inside but physically hauled her away to the home of Frank and his wife, Miranda.

"I'm sorry." The genuine compassion in Thad's soft voice brought tears to Susannah's eyes, blurring the brush and dead leaves covering the forest floor.

Not trusting her own voice, she only nodded and headed toward a nearby heap of rotting wood. In Thad's silence, she sensed he understood that the dozen years since her parents' deaths had not diminished the pain of her loss.

"Ruben's father is your only sibling, then?" He crouched to harvest another crop of mushrooms.

Susannah silently blessed him for not lingering on her sad memory. "No, my sister, Becky, and brother Jacob, and their families live in Madison. My brother-in-law, Ephraim, is a doctor there, and Jacob is a minister."

Thad's smiling, upturned face looked almost angelic caught in a sunbeam shafting through the forest canopy. "Ah, Madison is a lovely town. A couple of years ago while on railroad business, I had an occasion to visit Mr. Lanier's home there." His smile stretched wider. "I may have unknowingly passed your siblings on the broad thoroughfare of Main Cross Street."

The fact that he seemed to seek even so tenuous a connection between them caused her heart to mimic the hammering *rat-a-tats* of a nearby woodpecker.

In their long-exchanged look, Susannah felt as if she might melt into his pewter gaze. The almost tangible attraction between them set off warning bells inside her. She wrenched her gaze away to break the spell.

I must be daft! How could I even imagine. . .

Thad cleared his throat. His casual tone could not disguise an uncharacteristic tightness in his voice. "Naomi reminded me of the church social on Sunday afternoon a week from tomorrow to welcome the new minister and his family. I thought maybe. . ."

Thad's voice faded from Susannah's consciousness as a sudden unease gripped her. Her senses became keenly acute. Her body tensed, and her gaze darted around the little woods.

Thad gripped her arm. "Susannah, what is it? What's wrong?"

"Georgiana," Susannah croaked through her fear-constricted throat. "I can't see her anywhere! Georgiana! Georgiana!"

No answer came except for the chirping of the birds.

five

Susannah dropped the basket of mushrooms and raced toward the clump of bluebells where she'd last noticed Georgiana watching a butterfly. Only a few discarded bluebells and yellow dandelion blossoms evidenced her daughter's recent presence.

Guilt poured over Susannah. "I should have been watching her more closely. I should have—"

"She can't have gone far. We'll find her." Thad's confident tone as he came up beside her helped tame the panic raging in Susannah's belly.

As she searched his face for reassurance, Susannah felt her guilt reconfigure itself into resentment. How could she have allowed Thad Sutton to distract her from the most important thing in her life—her daughter?

She shrugged his hand from her shoulder and welcomed the anger replacing her mind-numbing dread. "I'm holding you to that, Captain Sutton," she said, fixing him with a glare.

Susannah felt a prick of remorse when he dropped his gaze to the ground. *Georgiana is my responsibility. I shouldn't be blaming anyone else. . . .*

Thad crouched down. With his finger, he traced an indention that looked like a tiny shoe print in the dark, sticky mud. Rising, he grasped her hand and with long, purposeful strides began hauling her through the woods. "She's gone this way."

Susannah ignored the brambles clutching at her skirt and the branches whipping near her face. As they emerged into the meadow, she frantically scanned the grassy expanse between the woods and the canal.

No Georgiana.

Thad paused. His intent gaze turned northwest toward the canal, and Susannah's heart jumped to her throat.

"Surely she hasn't—I've told her so many times..."

He answered by towing her across the meadow, his gaze fixed on what seemed to Susannah an indiscernible path through knee-high grass and wildflowers.

Susannah prayed Thad knew what he was doing as she struggled to keep up. Exertion and fear robbed her breath, rendering her unable to call out her daughter's name.

When they came upon two young boys baiting fishhooks near the canal's edge, Thad stopped. "Have you seen a little girl?"

"Georgiana," Susannah gasped, catching her breath. "Have you seen Georgiana?"

The boys, whom she recognized as Alex Milton and Davy McLeod, dropped their willow poles. Nodding, they turned wide eyes and guilty expressions toward her and Thad.

"Saw her up by the feeder dam." Alex pointed a grimy finger westward toward the dam that supplied the canal with water from a reservoir fed by the Whitewater River. "Hey, you won't tell our folks you saw us here, will ya? Cause we're s'posed to be..."

A distant splash jerked Susannah and Thad's attention from the boys and sent them sprinting toward the dam.

Oh, Lord, no! Please, no! The words tore from Susannah's terror-squeezed heart.

She stood shaking near the canal's edge, dimly aware that she'd just prayed her first heartfelt prayer in months.

The tranquil sound of the falling water sluicing over the dam into the canal only heightened her fear. Last summer she'd had Ruben teach Georgiana to swim in case she ever fell into the canal. But here, with the constant pouring of water into the canal, she feared her baby would be relentlessly pounded beneath the surface.

Without a word, Thad divested himself of his boots, socks,

and shirt and slid down the muddy bank. The four-feet-deep water came only to his midchest.

Susannah held her breath along with Thad as he dipped his face beneath the churning surface near the dam. Soon, he completely disappeared beneath the swirling white water.

An eternity seemed to pass while he remained submerged. She couldn't imagine how he'd held his breath so long. At last, he came up gasping for air and shaking his head, sending water droplets flying. "She's not here."

His pronouncement set Susannah's frantic heart oscillating between relief and dread.

Thad scrambled up the slippery bank. For a moment he stood looking west, beyond the lock, then east, toward the inn. "Come on." He fit the words between deep breaths as he snatched his shirt, socks, and boots from the muddy towpath and turned toward the inn.

Susannah struggled to match his long-legged strides. What had he seen? Was it just a hunch? She fought hysteria and the urge to jump into the canal and slosh a mile of its length in search of her baby.

As they neared the basin and Garrett Heywood's packet, Susannah perked her ears, and her heart began to race. Had she truly heard Georgiana's musical giggles wafting from the *Flying Eagle?*

"Georgiana! Georgiana!" Susannah leaped to the deck of the canal boat as she called her daughter's name.

"Hey, Susannah! This what you're lookin' for?" Smiling, Garrett emerged from the interior of the boat, carrying Georgiana. His cinnamon brown eyes sparkled beneath his shock of russet hair. "When I saw Georgiana, I figured you must be close by." He gave her a flirtatious wink.

They'd been playing this little cat and mouse game for the better part of a year, and Susannah had long grown weary of it. Ten years or so her senior, she had to admit Garrett Heywood, in his midthirties, was still quite a looker. But her feelings for him had never grown beyond friendship, and she doubted they ever would—especially while he continued to live the rather rowdy life of a canaler.

She ignored his wink, turning her attention to her daughter. "Georgiana, you had us sick with worry! Whatever possessed you to take off like that?" Wilting with relief, Susannah sagged against the outside wall of the canal boat's cabin.

Perched on the crook of Garrett's arm, Georgiana blinked at the reprimand while she clung to his neck and munched a sugar cookie as big as a man's hand. "I couldn't find you and Tad. T'ought you went home," she explained around a bite of cookie, sending golden crumbs showering onto Garrett's green coat.

Sallie O'Donnell, Garrett's canal boat cook, appeared from inside the boat. She pushed her straggling brown hair from her concerned face. "I'm right sorry if we caused you to fret, Missus Killion. I reckon it's my fault yer young'un's here."

The woman wadded the hem of her apron in her hands, an apologetic tone edging her words. "The child smelled my sugar cookies and asked Captain Heywood if she could have one. He brought her onto the boat fearin' she'd fall into the canal." She shot a nervous glance toward Garrett. "The captain would have carried her back to the inn directly, but I couldn't find it in me to deny her a cookie. I hope you don't mind me givin' her the treat."

"No—no, of course not. Thank you for looking after her." Susannah shot Sallie an unsteady smile and reached out trembling arms to take Georgiana from Garrett. "We were just frightened when we lost track of her in the woods. . . mushroom hunting."

Surprise joined the relief flooding through Susannah. She'd never heard the reclusive Widow O'Donnell string more than three or four words together. Though still a young woman—in her early thirties, Susannah guessed—Sallie generally kept to herself when in Promise. The only exception being her faithful attendance at worship services as Garrett docked the *Flying Eagle* here in Promise from Saturday evening until he headed the boat back toward Cincinnati early each Monday morning. But even at church, the retiring woman rarely socialized. Because of her timid manner, many folks in Promise considered Sallie O'Donnell a bit odd.

"Little early in the season to go for a swim in the canal, ain't it, Captain Sutton?" Garrett narrowed his eyes toward Thad, who'd replaced his shirt and boots and stood dripping puddles of water onto the towpath from his drenched breeches.

An easy grin quirked Thad's mouth. "We feared Georgiana had fallen into the canal. Two boys sent us down to the dam when we inquired if they'd seen her."

Garrett gave a quick chuckle that turned into a snort. "Young Milton and McLeod. Their paps'll give 'em a good hidin' if they catch 'em skippin' school to go fishin'."

Switching subjects, he fixed Thad with a cold glare. "Mushroom huntin', huh? Find any? Don't see a sack."

"We left the sacks in the woods when we noticed Georgiana was missing." Susannah snapped the terse reply as indignation stiffened her back. Was Garrett suggesting anything improper between her and Thad? How dare he even imply such a thing!

"I'll tell you what I *did* find, Captain Heywood." All humor had evaporated from Thad's face and voice. "While in the canal down by the feeder dam, I noticed the thing is riddled with muskrat burrows. Worse, they've compromised the towpath bank."

Thad cocked his head in the direction of the dam then pinned Garrett with a stare. "The ground is near saturation." His voice lowered as concern etched his brow. "One good rainy spell and both the dam and much of the canal bank will likely crumble and half of Promise will be flooded. I suggest the entire stretch from the dam to the basin be shut down immediately for repairs."

A concerned look flitted briefly across Garrett's face before his expression hardened again. "Maybe. And maybe you just want another reason to put this canal out of business. . .Captain Sutton." Thad's name dripped with scorn from Garrett Heywood's lips.

Even if Thad's appraisal of the canal's condition gave Garrett pause, Susannah knew Garrett would never accept a railroad man's word without checking for himself.

Thad's posture stiffened, and the muscles worked in his jaw. "Now listen here, Heywood, are you calling me a liar? Maybe you don't care about this town, but a lot of other people do."

Concerned by the escalating tension, Susannah turned to the canal boat cook. Perhaps by injecting a new topic, she could break up the men's verbal sparring match before it turned to fisticuffs. "Sallie—that is your name, isn't it?" she asked in a bright voice.

Looking as uneasy as Susannah felt, the O'Donnell woman gave her a shy nod.

"Are you planning to attend the church social a week from tomorrow, Sallie? My mother-in-law, Naomi, is on the organization committee." Susannah fully expected a negative response from the woman, but at least Thad and Garrett had stopped arguing.

"I'd thought I might." Sallie murmured the startling reply and swiped a strand of hair from her brow.

"Actually," Garrett barged into the conversation, "I was thinkin' I might go, too. Sounds like some good eats, and Sallie is always pesterin' me to go to church." He dipped a quick bow toward Susannah. "But I'll only go if you'll allow me to squire you to the event, Susannah."

Stunned, Susannah almost dropped Georgiana. She'd never known Garrett to darken the door of a church, at least not in Promise.

"Well. . .I. . ." Susannah tried to think of a way out of this uncomfortable position. She certainly didn't want to encourage Garrett's attentions. But although her own faith had waned, it bothered her to discourage an unsaved soul from being exposed to the scriptures. "Yes—yes, of course, Captain Heywood. I'll be happy to accompany you."

She didn't dare look at Thad as her attention shifted from Garrett's self-satisfied grin back to Sallie. "And I look forward to seeing you there, too, Sallie." If Sallie did attend, her presence could provide a buffer between her and Garrett. But Susannah's hope of that happening dwindled when the woman gave a noncommittal shrug and ducked back into the boat.

During their walk back to the inn, Georgiana's happy chatter filled the uneasy silence stretching between Susannah and Thad. Susannah suspected Thad had been about to ask her to the social before they realized Georgiana was missing.

"We forgot the mushwooms and gweens. Tad, you're not listening!" Nestled securely in Thad's arms, Georgiana tugged on his sleeve.

The frown that had cleft his brow dissolved, and his lips lifted in a smile. "Don't worry, moppet. I'll go back to the woods and fetch them."

When they reached the oak tree behind the inn, Thad lowered Georgiana to the ground then glanced at the sun riding high in the eastern sky. "It must be nearly ten o'clock," he said, giving Georgiana a serious look. "Didn't you tell me your dolly takes her tea at ten o'clock sharp, moppet?"

"Ohhh!" Georgiana's eyes widened and she pressed her fingers to her lips. "Dolly will be cwoss," she muttered before whirling around and scampering off toward the inn's kitchen door.

When her daughter disappeared inside the building, Susannah turned to Thad. "You're very good with her."

His lips tipped up. "She's a sweet child. I like her a lot."

Suddenly, Susannah blurted the question that had scratched at her mind since Thad's argument with Garrett. "Do you really think the canal is in danger of collapsing?" The memory of past floods made her want to believe Garrett was right and

Thad simply aimed to impugn the canal. But if that were true, it meant Thad was less than honest—a notion she found more than a little disheartening.

"Yes, I do." His answer came without hesitation, and his gaze never flinched from hers.

Susannah nodded somberly. She believed him. And that made her glad, despite learning of the canal's instability. But worrying about the canal would have to wait. She'd had enough worry for one day.

Taking in Thad's bedraggled condition, a new wave of gratitude rolled through her. "Thank you for helping me find Georgiana. I'm glad you were with us. I don't know what I would have done if I'd been alone and lost track of her. . . ."

"You would have managed just fine, I have no doubt."

The respect shining in his gray eyes set Susannah's heart singing ridiculously.

"I want you to know I enjoyed this morning very much— except, of course, for the scare with Georgiana," he added, the corner of his mouth dimpling with his grin.

Warmth flooded Susannah's cheeks. She turned her face askance in an attempt to hide her blush. "Thank you, too, for offering to fetch the sacks of greens and mushrooms. You may leave them on the worktable in the kitchen," she murmured and stepped toward the inn.

"Susannah. . ." His quiet voice stopped her, turning her around and sending her pulse racing again. "I was going to ask you. . .you know, to the church social."

"I know." She gave him a weak smile. "I hope you will still come—for Naomi's sake."

"Wouldn't miss it." He cast the parting comment brightly over his shoulder then headed for the meadow.

Disappointment skittered through Susannah as she walked back to the inn. There was nothing more to say. Garrett had beat Thad to the invitation, and she had accepted. Perhaps it was better this way. Though potentially aggravating, a Sunday afternoon spent in the company of Garrett Heywood would not be as unsettling as one spent in the company of Captain Thad Sutton. Yes, perhaps it was better this way.

At the kitchen door, she turned and gazed across the meadow at Thad's stalwart figure striding toward the woods through the knee-deep expanse of grass and wildflowers. Leaning against the doorjamb, she heaved a soft sigh.

So why doesn't it feel better?

six

The horse neighed and jerked its head in protest as Thad yanked the harness belly cinch tight.

"Sorry about that, boy." He patted the glossy black side of the animal's head. It wasn't this poor creature's fault that Thad had allowed Garrett Heywood to beat him out of enjoying Susannah's company at the church social.

Thad remembered how Heywood had shown up early in a rented buggy to escort Susannah and Georgiana to church, and a streak of jealousy shot through him.

As consolation, Thad had offered to escort Naomi to Sunday services as well as the social immediately following. Although shorter and slighter built than his aunt Edith, Naomi Killion's personality reminded him of his beloved relative.

A wry grin twisted his mouth. He could use some of Aunt Edith's comforting hugs and homespun wisdom about now.

Grasping the leather bridle strap, he led the horse with its attached buggy to the inn's side door. The dull sound of the horse's plodding clops on the dirt path echoed Thad's drab mood.

A moment after he brought the rig to a halt, Naomi appeared at the inn's open door with a baking pan swathed in linen. "Captain Sutton, it's so nice of you to drive me to church."

"Here, let me take that for you." He relieved her lace-gloved hands of the pan.

"You are a true blessing, Captain." Heaving a sigh, she gave him a grateful look. "Besides this pan of cornbread, Susannah and I have prepared two pies and a basketful of fried chicken for the social. Garrett Heywood had no room to transport any

44

of it in that little rented shay, and Ruben left on horseback to fetch that Macklin girl he's sweet on."

Thad deposited the pan of cornbread in the storage box at the rear of the buggy then followed Naomi into the inn.

The spry little woman hurried to the kitchen, her silky black skirt whispering as she walked. "I don't reckon this is quite the way you'd envisioned your Sunday morning, is it?" She grinned, her quick hands deftly wrapping linen towels around apple and rhubarb pies.

Thad couldn't help inhaling the delicious aromas that greeted him at the kitchen door. "Actually, I've been looking forward to the social since last Sunday when you first invited me—"

"You know that's not what I meant, Captain Sutton." Naomi gave him a knowing grin, thrusting a little hamper that smelled of fried chicken toward him.

Thad accepted the hamper, unsure how to answer. Surely she didn't expect him to admit his disappointment at missing Susannah's company.

"Well, I. . ." He searched for something evasive to say but failed to form any intelligent thought.

Naomi swished past him, a pie in each hand. "It's not exactly the day she'd planned either, you know." She tossed the statement over her shoulder as they exited the inn.

Thad nestled the pies and chicken beside the cornbread then helped Naomi into the buggy. He'd have to watch himself. Like Aunt Edith, the woman seemed adept at reading his mind.

They rolled along Sycamore Street in congenial silence. Above them, the trees for which the street had been named reached out a canopy of graceful branches beginning to fill out with young green leaves. A warm spring breeze carried the fragrance of lilacs to Thad's nostrils and fluttered the ends of his carefully tied cravat. A red-winged blackbird called out a salutation as they passed its fence post perch.

Thad wished he felt as tranquil as the spring morning.

Although thoughts of Susannah dominated his mind, he was reluctant to voice those private musings to her mother-in-law. However, mindful of his extended reticence, Thad gave the lady beside him a sidelong glance. He felt compelled to inject some subject of conversation.

Suddenly, he realized he'd never personally offered Naomi his sympathy concerning George's death. "I fear I have never sufficiently extended my condolences in regard to your son's passing. I'd like to rectify that now, however belated." A tiny ball of anxiety wound in his belly as he wondered how she would respond to both the subject and the oversight.

Naomi's pleasant expression softened to a kind smile. She touched his arm. "Captain Sutton, your eloquent letter four years ago was more than sufficient."

Thad's fingers tightened on the reins. "George was a brave and loyal soldier."

Naomi's blue eyes glistened, but her smile never wavered. "He would have been."

Thad marveled at her serenity. "How have you been able to accept it when. . ."

"When Susannah can't?" She fixed him with that look that seemed to see more than he'd like and made him want to squirm. "I know my boy's in the arms of Jesus. 'And we know that all things work together for good to them that love God, to them who are the called according to his purpose,' " she quoted.

"Susannah doesn't believe that?" Thad guided the horse left, down Laurel Street, toward the churchyard.

"Oh, she believes it. . .deep down." Weary regret tinged Naomi's tone. "Susannah's and George's lives were twisted together since they were little. I think it's just easier for her to be angry with God than to open her heart and look for His greater purpose in her life."

Naomi shook her head sadly. "I'm not sure she's ever really faced George's death. I think she shoved it all back into a dark cubbyhole in her heart and threw herself into running the inn and raising Georgiana." She shot him a grin. "I'm afraid I have no head for business. I must confess Susannah is the reason we have managed to keep the inn open."

Thad pulled on the reins, bringing the buggy to a stop beside the little stone and clapboard church. Contemplating Naomi's words, he jumped to the ground and tied the horse to the hitching post. Had Susannah's heart died with George, or might it be possible for someone else to rekindle a new purpose in it?

When he helped Naomi from the buggy, Thad's gaze wandered to the church's side yard. Susannah and Heywood, with Georgiana at their heels, giggled together while they worked with several others to set up the food tables. He frowned, almost hoping Naomi was right and Susannah's heart remained closed to the notion of a new love.

"If she'd wanted Heywood for a husband, she could have had him six times over this past year."

At Naomi's words, Thad felt heat march up his neck. The woman did see more than he would like. Not trusting his voice, he offered her his arm.

As they mounted the church steps, his face turned unbidden toward the side yard. He saw Susannah playfully smack Heywood's hand when he snatched a tablecloth from her.

A weight like a cannonball seemed to lodge in Thad's chest, and he felt Naomi give his arm two soft pats.

Yes, the woman sees far too much.

At this moment, however, that realization was somehow comforting.

❧

In the churchyard, Susannah smoothed a bunched corner of the quilt she'd spread on the shady grass beneath a flowering tulip poplar tree. She'd staked out the spot earlier while helping to set up the trestle tables for the food. If the picnic's location was ideal, her companion for the occasion certainly wasn't.

Garrett Heywood had seemed uncomfortable during the church service. He'd sat across the aisle from her on the men's side of the church, and his constant fidgeting had raked down her nerves like a flax carder. She'd found his deportment a stark contrast to Thad Sutton's attentive reverence.

Thad Sutton.

Susannah looked toward the hitching posts near the front of the church and watched Thad hand Naomi a linen-swathed pie. The ever-present war of emotions raged inside her. If Thad Sutton's railroad replaced the canal, it spelled the end of the Killion House Inn. Yet that knowledge didn't prevent her from wishing she'd be sharing this picnic spot with Thad instead of with Garrett. So her heart fluttered when she saw Naomi and Thad making their way toward her after depositing the food on the tables.

Georgiana, who'd been bouncing beside Thad like a happy puppy, skipped to her. "Mamma, I told Tad and Gwamma to bwing their quilt over here by you," she said, plopping down on the quilt, a pink puddle of calico skirt splaying around her.

Naomi bustled up, a crazy quilt draped across her arm. "What a perfect patch of shady yard, Susannah. Do you mind if Captain Sutton and I share it with you?"

"No, of course not." Silently blessing her mother-in-law, Susannah hurried to help Naomi spread out her quilt. Since Sallie O'Donnell had refused her invitation to sit with her and Garrett, Susannah welcomed the extra company.

"Georgiana insisted we all eat together," Thad explained with a grin that sent Susannah's heart into silly somersaults.

"I think that is a wonderful idea," Susannah said in a rush. But when she cast a glance at Garrett, who was striding toward them, a new concern bloomed. His frown suggested he didn't share her sentiment. She worried that unfriendly sparks would fly again between the two men.

"Mrs. Killion." Unsmiling, Garrett dipped a stiff bow in Naomi's direction then turned to Thad. "Captain Sutton." His voice hardening, he spared Thad a quick nod but didn't offer his hand.

Susannah's stomach knotted as she watched the two men's glares cross rapiers for an instant. News of Thad's business in Promise had spread like a grass fire in August. She'd heard the angry grumbles around town. Even before the Whitewater Canal had been dug, the town had sprung up on the promise of its coming—giving birth to the town's name. So the presence of someone who threatened to take away its reason to exist raised the community's collective hackles.

She also understood Garrett's personal concern. He'd built up a fairly profitable packet business that ran weekly between Cincinnati and Promise. If a railroad turned the canal into a useless ditch, he stood to lose as much as she, or anyone else in Promise.

When the preacher gave the invocation from his spot in the center of the churchyard, Susannah struggled to keep her mind off her worries and on Pastor Ezekiel Murdoch's words.

She actually liked the new minister, finding him exceedingly personable. A robust man of some fifty-odd years, he possessed a hearty laugh, a jolly disposition, and an eloquent oratory fueled by a fiery zeal.

But his message today from the first chapter of Second Corinthians extolling God's promises to comfort the suffering had echoed hollowly in her ears. God had promised to answer her prayers, yet so many times His answer had been, "No."

She glanced at Thad, handing Georgiana a tin plate. Now, in a seemingly cruel twist of circumstance, the man who would snatch away her livelihood also made her heart misbehave.

Folks filled their plates from the vast array of dishes covering several trestle tables.

Carrying both her and Georgiana's plates of food, Susannah joined the others around the quilts. There, Naomi took charge of Georgiana, leaving Susannah stuck between Thad and Garrett.

Thad hurried to assist Susannah with her plate, and Garrett held her glass of tea while she situated herself on the quilt. Taking extra time to carefully adjust her ivory-colored cotton skirt around her, Susannah hoped to extend the uneasy truce between Thad and Garrett. But the moment she'd settled her plate on her lap and had her glass of tea in hand, the men began their verbal sparring.

"Really, Sutton, I don't see any need for a railroad now that the canal is operational again." Sitting cross-legged beside her, Garrett poked a fork at his potato salad with a ferocity that suggested he'd rather poke the utensil into Thaddeus Sutton's ribs.

"But for how long?" Thad picked up the chicken leg from his tin plate and jabbed it in the general direction of the canal. "As you've experienced, one good flood renders the thing unusable."

Although it irked her to do so, Susannah felt compelled to come to Garrett's assistance. "But they fixed the canal," she said and was rewarded by an appreciative smile from Garrett.

Thad shook his head and frowned. "Not from what I've witnessed. I've already told you about the muskrat damage I noticed near the feeder dam. Hard telling how many other places along the bank have been compromised."

Garrett snorted in reply.

For the next several minutes, a strained silence reigned while they ate. At length, Naomi rose. "If you'll excuse me, I think I'll go have a word with Pastor Murdoch and his wife."

Susannah knew Naomi avoided discord whenever possible, but she couldn't help wondering if Naomi, too, was bothered by Thad's opinion of the canal's instability. Whatever the case, Susannah envied Naomi's opportunity to walk away from the unsettling conversation.

"I'm all done," Georgiana declared, wiping the back of her hand across her mouth. Making her way over to Susannah, she crawled into her mother's lap and snuggled.

Susannah rocked her daughter in her arms, reveling in her child's baby softness. Tears stung her eyelids as she nuzzled her face against Georgiana's blond curls. At four years old, Georgiana was fast approaching an age when she would no longer care to cuddle.

Garrett mumbled something about rhubarb pie and headed for the food tables.

Thad sat still, a tender expression softening the angles of his face. His gentle smile as he watched her hold her child touched a deep, warm place inside Susannah.

"Pastor Murdoch seems to have been very well received here," Susannah said, trying to find a subject of conversation that had nothing to do with the Whitewater Canal or Thad's business in Promise.

Thad followed her gaze to the church's front yard enclosed in white pickets. There, Pastor Murdoch and his plump wife stood visiting with several parishioners, including Naomi. "Yes, Promise is lucky to have him. I can't remember when I've heard such an inspiring sermon."

Susannah couldn't think of an appropriate, yet honest, response. Dismayed, she realized she'd unwittingly steered the conversation to another uncomfortable topic.

As she grappled for a reply, a boy of about six, whom she recognized as the miller's youngest son, stepped toward them. He glanced shyly from his dusty shoe tops to their faces and back again.

"We're playing ring-around-the-rosy. May Georgiana play, too?"

"Where?" Susannah darted a quick look about the church-yard. She wouldn't want to send Georgiana out of her field of vision or among children too much older than her daughter.

"Over there." The boy pointed to a group of children of varying ages gathered in a grassy meadow several yards beyond the food tables. "I'll take care of her and see she doesn't get hurt or dirty."

"Good man," Thad said, the corner of his mouth twitching.

"Pease, Mamma, pease!" Georgiana pushed away from Susannah and jumped up from her lap.

"I suppose." These were all children with whom Georgiana regularly attended Sunday school. Susannah eyed the children playing in the distance and started to get up. "It's quite a ways away. Maybe I should go. . ."

Thad stood. "You stay. I'll handle this reconnaissance." He turned a serious face to Georgiana. "What do you think, moppet? Shall we go join the maneuvers?" At Georgiana's affirming nod, he swung the giggling child to his shoulders and gave the boy a smart salute. "Lead on, soldier." The quick wink he cast over his shoulder to Susannah sent her heart tumbling.

Garrett called her name twice before Susannah wrenched her attention from the sight of Thad striding across the churchyard with Georgiana perched atop his shoulders.

"I took the liberty of bringin' you a piece of cherry pie for dessert. I remember you mentionin' once that it was your favorite."

"Thank you, Garrett." Susannah accepted the dessert dish and gave him a wobbly smile.

He lowered himself beside her on the quilt. "Now that we're alone, I've been meanin' to ask you somethin' real important." He seemed to study the piece of rhubarb pie on his dessert dish. "I know it can't be easy, bein' a widow woman and all. . . ."

Panic grabbed at Susannah's chest. She should have known he'd eventually get around to this, yet she found herself unprepared. "Garrett, don't. I mean. . .Naomi and I are doing fine, and we have Ruben. . . ."

Garrett shook his head. "Your nephew's a fine boy. But it ain't like havin' a man of your own."

Susannah gave his arm a gentle squeeze. "You're a dear friend, and I appreciate your concern. I really do. But I'm not sure I'll ever marry again."

The sound of children's laughter turned her face toward the meadow, and her gaze lit upon the figure of Thad Sutton.

Garrett's look followed hers, and his voice hardened, taking on a sharp edge. "Maybe you will, and maybe you won't. But just remember who cares about what's important to you— your inn and the Whitewater Canal!"

Leaving his piece of pie untouched, Garrett sprang up and strode away, disappearing behind the church.

Susannah rose and heaved a frustrated sigh. Garrett was a good friend, and she hated to hurt him. She noticed Sallie O'Donnell scowling from across the churchyard where she sat with several older widows. Susannah wondered if Garrett had mentioned to his cook that he intended to propose and Sallie surmised by his actions that he'd been refused.

Deciding she should at least try to soothe Garrett's wounded feelings, she headed behind the church. But as she neared the back corner of the building, the sound of Ruben's distraught voice stopped her cold.

"I'm sorry, Lilly. I know it's all my fault. I—I could marry you."

Lilly drew an audibly ragged breath. "I'm not sure I'm ready to marry. I'm only fifteen. But my dad. . .my dad. . ." Her words faded to muffled sobs. Although the couple remained out of her line of vision, Susannah imagined Ruben muffling Lilly's sobs against his chest.

Susannah knew she shouldn't continue listening but found herself rooted to the ground, anger and concern twisting through her like a hot poker. For the first time, she began to regret having taken in her brother's son when he appeared at the inn two years ago.

The eldest of Frank's children, Ruben had no interest in or aptitude for his father's blacksmith trade, which had caused constant friction between the two and prompted the boy to run away from home. And because Susannah provided Ruben sanctuary rather than sending him back to his parents in Hamilton County, she'd angered her brother. Although she'd had no further communication with Frank, she had received a letter from Ruben's mother, Miranda, thanking her for taking Ruben in and asking her to look after him. And so she had—or had at least tried to.

Frank and Miranda had trusted her with their son, and she'd let them down. Hugging her arms around her trembling body, Susannah's pulse pounded in her head. She felt sick.

seven

Dawn stained the inn's kitchen with a rosy hue. Susannah yawned as she pitched another piece of kindling into the flaming belly of the cookstove and clanged the door shut. Sleep had been fitful.

She hadn't confronted Ruben with what she'd heard or mentioned it to Naomi. If what she suspected was true, it would come to light soon enough.

When she'd first walked into the kitchen, she'd glanced out the window and barely made out the white form of the *Flying Eagle* gliding away from the inn, down the canal's dark trough.

Usually Garrett stayed long enough on Monday mornings to take his breakfast at the inn before heading back to Cincinnati. This morning, she supposed she couldn't blame him for choosing Sallie's canal boat fare instead.

She had no regrets about turning down Garrett's proposal or, more accurately, stopping him before he finished proposing. Yet, his words had played through her mind all night. *"Remember who cares about what's important to you—your inn and the Whitewater Canal."*

Susannah snatched a bag of flour from the pantry. She slammed it down hard on the kitchen worktable, sending up a plume of white dust. Garrett was right. If the man who made her heart dance cared one jot about her, Naomi, or Georgiana, why didn't he pack up his surveyor's gear and leave the Whitewater Canal alone?

He *didn't* care.

She mixed the biscuit dough with ferocious hands, squeezing until the sticky stuff oozed through her fingers. If only she could squeeze Thad Sutton from her mind—and her heart.

The sound of Thad's bright whistle sent a flame of anger spiraling through her, puckering her forehead in a scowl.

He strode through the kitchen doorway and glanced toward her, and the happy tune fell silent. "Sorry, I didn't mean to disturb anyone. I was wondering if Master Ruben might be up and about. I could really use a pole man today."

Susannah frowned at the lump of dough she patted on the table's floured surface. "I haven't seen him. But as he seems careless about how his actions affect others, he'll probably be willing to help you." She punctuated her ambiguous comment with jabs to the innocent biscuit dough.

Thad's left eyebrow shot up. Then, blowing out a long breath, he set his transit case on the floor and stepped closer. "Look, Susannah, what I'm doing here is not personal, nor do I have any sort of feud with the canal. But change is coming. And if you, Heywood, and the rest of the people in Promise don't prepare for the change, it could be a jolt."

"A jolt?" Susannah shoved flour-covered hands against her hips. "Garrett could probably take his boat to the Erie or Wabash Canals, and the farmers and mill owners could transport their products to the nearest train depot." She tapped her chest. "But what am I to do? If the railroad decides to bypass Promise by placing a passenger depot at Connersville or Metamora, the Killion House Inn is done."

He had the decency to look embarrassed. "There's always the National Road traffic, and you have my promise I'll do all in my power to encourage the railroad to place a depot here."

Susannah rammed a tin cup down on the dough, twisted it, and cut out a biscuit. She plopped it in a baking pan then pinned him with a glare.

"Each time the canal has been down and we've had to depend on only the National Road traffic, we've barely made ends meet. A railroad will cut into the stagecoach traffic, too, drawing away travelers who are foolhardy, curious about train travel, or just plain impatient." She fought the fear that crawled up her chest and clutched at her throat. "And like I told you before, I don't put much store in promises."

The amber rays of the morning sun highlighted the muscles working in his angular jaw. He strode stiffly out the kitchen door and didn't return to the inn for breakfast or dinner.

Her contentious exchange with Thad Sutton hung heavily on Susannah's conscience throughout the day. Even now, as the afternoon shadows stretched across the inn's backyard and she took down Monday's washing from the clothesline, she couldn't divest herself of the guilt prickling at the back of her mind. She knew everything he'd told her made sense. But every day he worked to map a way for the hated rails marked a day closer to the demise of the Killion House Inn.

If he'd just go away. . .

If he went away. . .what? She would feel better?

No.

Susannah grasped the corner of a billowing sheet, freeing it from the wooden pins that anchored it to the line. If only she could get Thad Sutton and his railroad off her mind. The next moment, her wish was granted in the most unexpected way.

"Aunt Susannah?"

Susannah whirled at Ruben's quiet voice. She felt heat rush to her face. Had Ruben noticed her in the churchyard yesterday? Did he suspect that she'd heard his conversation with Lilly Macklin?

"Ruben, what is it?" Her sorry attempt at a light tone came out a nervous squeak.

"I have something real important I need to ask you." Ruben crushed the brim of his black felt hat in hands larger than a sixteen-year-old boy should have. His stocky build, broad shoulders, and wavy auburn hair reminded Susannah of her brother Frank. But in his dark eyes glancing anxiously from her face to his boot tops, Susannah saw the shy, sensitive eyes of his mother, Miranda.

"Wha–what?" Her limbs going noodle-weak, she dropped

the sheet and pins into the laundry basket. She walked to the oak tree and sank to the bench beneath it.

"I need to ask a favor." Ruben followed her and scuffed the toe of his boot in a bare patch of sandy loam. "Do you think maybe you could hire Lilly to help here at the inn?"

Susannah's mind raced. Was this Ruben's solution to his and Lilly's predicament? "Well, I don't know. . . ." Should she hire a girl in Lilly's condition? Beyond that, the inn had been doing financially better in the past few months but certainly not well enough to pay for extra help.

"Thing is"—anger clouded Ruben's handsome boyish features—"her pap's been beatin' her real reg'lar the last couple months. He don't like it none that we've been keepin' company." His dark, soulful eyes met hers. "She needs someplace else to live—someplace where she'll be safe."

Susannah rubbed her throbbing temple. She couldn't allow Lilly to continue being abused, especially if she was in the family way. Yet, it didn't change the fact that she really couldn't afford a hired girl. George's father had borrowed two-thirds of the money from the bank to buy and furnish the inn. Next month, another installment would be due on that loan. "I don't know, Ruben. We can't afford to pay a hired girl—"

"You don't have to pay her. Like me, she'll work for room and board. She'll be a lot of help. She can watch Georgiana when you and Naomi have other things to do." His brown eyes glistened, and the plea in his voice crumpled her resistance.

"All right." Susannah managed a weak smile.

Ruben's face split with a toothy grin, and he grabbed Susannah in a hug that snatched away her breath. "Thanks, Aunt Susannah!" He planted a quick kiss on her cheek. "You won't be sorry, I promise!"

Susannah watched her nephew sprint to the front of the inn and across the National Road in the general direction of Macklin's Sawmill. Her insides churned with trepidation. *Another promise.*

❧

Susannah started up the stairway with a load of clean bed linens. Two weeks had passed since Lilly's arrival at the inn, and Susannah was glad to admit that Ruben had been right. The slight, shy girl worked tirelessly each day from dawn until dusk, cheerfully doing whatever was asked of her without so much as a pout.

Susannah and Naomi had both stifled gasps when Ruben first escorted Lilly into the inn's kitchen, toting a brown calico sack filled with her few belongings. An ugly purple bruise darkened a quarter-moon shaped area beneath her left eye and puffed up her discolored cheek. She'd draped a broad swath of her strawberry blond hair across her face as if attempting to hide the injury. The sight made Susannah glad she'd given in to Ruben's plea.

It amazed Susannah how quickly and seamlessly Lilly fit into the routine of the inn. The girl seemed mature beyond her fifteen years, and Susannah enjoyed the daily company of another young woman. Their employer-to-employee relationship quickly evaporated, replaced by a warmer, almost sisterly friendship.

Susannah had been both thrilled and relieved by Lilly's discreetly whispered question one afternoon shortly after her arrival. The girl had sidled up to her in the kitchen's pantry closet and confided that she was on her monthly and needed to know the location of the clean rags used for such occasions.

A surge of guilt had quickly swamped Susannah's initial relief. Realizing she'd sadly misjudged Ruben and Lilly, Susannah vowed to try and put a little extra money aside to pay them each a small salary.

Georgiana, too, had taken to the girl immediately, and Lilly seemed to enjoy spending time with the child as well. Susannah noticed that her daughter's speech improved after Lilly began making a game of helping Georgiana with her pronunciations.

On her way to one of the guest rooms, Susannah stopped in the hallway when she caught sight of Georgiana helping Lilly make a bed.

Georgiana plunged her little fists into the ends of a pillow. "Just like the story you told me about the three bears, Lilly, this pillow will be just wite!"

Lilly grinned, her brows shooting up. "Just what?"

Georgiana shook her head. "I meant right."

Lilly gave Georgiana a quick hug. "That's six this afternoon! You pronounce your *th* sounds and *r*'s correctly four more times today, and I'll read you another fairy story."

Smiling, Susannah stepped into the room, amazed at the improvement in Georgiana's enunciations. "Lilly, you are a born teacher," she said, giving the girl a hug. "I wanted to let you know"—Susannah brightened—"I can't promise anything, but I hope to be able to pay you a little at the end of the month. You've been such a wonderful help."

The unabashed joy shining from Lilly's face caused Susannah to wonder how long it had been since the motherless girl had heard a word of appreciation.

"Oh." A look of recollection lit Lilly's eyes, and she dug into her apron pocket. "Captain Sutton gave me this for taking such good care of his room." She held a half-dollar piece toward Susannah. "I thought I should give it to you—for the inn."

Georgiana skipped to Susannah. "Thad gave me money, too." She dipped her hand into her own apron pocket and pulled out a shiny penny.

Susannah shook her head at Lilly. "Captain Sutton meant for you to have it—not the inn. The railroad pays quite handsomely for him to board here. Even though he's often gone surveying for days on end," she added, disliking the wistful tone she heard in her voice.

The mention of Thad Sutton churned up troubling emotions in Susannah. She shifted her gaze to the open window overlooking the canal. After their argument in the kitchen two weeks ago, she'd seen little of him. Although she knew his work was taking him farther afield, she couldn't help wondering if their disagreement had something to do with his extended absences. If he had ever entertained special feelings for her, surely their impasse over the canal had squelched them.

"Me, too, Mamma?"

Georgiana's voice jerked Susannah's head around to her daughter, who proudly held up her penny.

"Yes, Georgiana." Susannah smiled at her child's hopeful look. "In fact, I think you should put it in your piggy bank right now before you lose it."

"He asked after you," Lilly said quietly when Georgiana had scampered from the room.

Susannah's cheeks tingled as heat spread up from her neck. "Who?" she asked in a voice she hoped sounded casual.

Lilly lifted the load of linens from Susannah's arms. "You know very well 'who.' Captain Sutton, that's who."

"Is there something the captain requires?" Susannah ignored the teasing lilt in the girl's tone.

"By the way he looks at you since he returned to Promise, I'd say he requires your company, or at least, your good graces, if I might say so—"

"No, Lilly, you should not say so!" Susannah tried her hardest to sound stern. She realized she'd failed when Lilly answered her admonishment with a giggle.

"Anyway," Lilly said, her voice skipping over a chuckle, "I told him you are quite well but seemed a little sad and that maybe he should say a word or two to cheer you up."

Susannah's jaw went slack, aghast at the girl's audacity. "Lilly, surely you did not!" Susannah pressed her palm to her searing cheek. What if Thad thought she'd put Lilly up to making such a suggestion? It didn't bear thinking.

"I surely did"—Lilly lifted her chin—"and don't look so horrified. You know you're really glad."

"I am *not* glad!" The feeling bubbling inside Susannah disputed her claim. "And you must shoo such fanciful thoughts from your head and never do such a thing again, do you hear?"

"I hear." Seeming unfazed, Lilly cast a soft chuckle over her shoulder and headed for the next room.

Descending the stairs, Susannah's mind raced with her heart. She labored to recall a word or look she'd gotten recently from Thad Sutton that might support Lilly's claim. The harder she tried to shove the notion of Thad's affection from her mind, the more it possessed her thoughts. As she reached the bottom step, she was determined to pay particular attention to the man's demeanor the next time she saw him.

She turned the corner to head toward the kitchen and gasped when her face smacked against Thad's chest.

"Whoa, there!" His soft voice sounded breathless. His arms encircled her, steadying her from the jarring impact.

"I'm sorry," they said in unison then laughed.

Thad kept her captive in his arms far longer than necessary before letting her go and taking a jerky step backward.

"I *am* sorry, you know." The penitent look in his gray eyes suggested his comment was not confined to their silly collision.

"So am I," Susannah managed to mutter.

A sweet sadness gnarled around her heart as she headed for the kitchen. A bouquet of wishes sprang up in her breast, each wish-blossom fading quickly, like flowers picked in the heat of August. She wished Thad Sutton had never come to Promise. She wished she'd never heard of trains or railroads. But mostly she wished Lilly Macklin had been wrong.

eight

Thad stood at the window of his room, his mood as dark as the storm clouds assailing the glass with their relentless deluge. With a frustrated shove, he pushed the navy blue wool curtains away from the pane.

The rain had continued almost nonstop for nearly three days.

It wasn't his inability to do his surveying work that concerned him. In truth, he'd amassed close to half the data needed by the railroad. It was the sight of the swollen Whitewater Canal—now a raging torrent—that gripped him with a mounting unease.

Boats were still managing to navigate the bloated ditch. Two days ago, Garrett Heywood had deposited a boatful of sodden, ill-tempered passengers at the side door of the Killion House Inn. But Thad feared the *Flying Eagle* might be the last boat to make it to Promise for some time to come. Much more of this rain, and the muskrat-pocked canal walls would crumble for sure.

Thad let the curtain fall across the window, partially obscuring the depressing vista. He turned away from the glass as if ignoring the rain might make it stop.

Sinking to the blue and white patchwork quilt covering his feather bed, he rubbed his forehead. A regiment of worries rumbled through his mind like the jaw-jarring thunderclaps, making his head pound.

He wasn't the only one concerned. Yesterday afternoon he'd watched Susannah standing at the kitchen door, gazing at the burgeoning canal. The fear he'd seen flickering in her eyes left little doubt as to what thoughts had drawn her brow into a worried V. With the canal basin only feet from the inn's back door, an overflow could easily send floodwaters through the building's ground floor.

Thad couldn't remember when he'd felt so helpless. He'd wanted to take her in his arms and assure her he wouldn't allow anything bad to happen to her or her inn.

But he couldn't. He was but a mere man, and they were at the mercy of the Lord.

A flash of lightning lit the room, illuminating the blue-and-white-striped wallpaper and dark rag-rugs scattered across the bare floor.

He scanned the cozy little space that had been his home these past six weeks. Like its proprietors, this inn had become dear to him. Guilt drenched his heart as Susannah's words of two weeks ago echoed accusingly through his mind. *"If the railroad decides to bypass Promise by placing a passenger depot at Connersville or Metamora, the Killion House Inn is done."*

Thad knew it was far more likely that the railroad board would choose the larger town of Connersville over tiny Promise for a depot location. Now a flood threatened, and there was nothing he could do to stop it. Or was there?

His gaze drifted to his little black Bible on the bedside table. The Bible he'd carried with him to war on the Texas plains. The Bible he'd read from while standing over countless graves—including George Killion's.

Another wave of guilt rippled through him. He'd taken so much from Susannah Killion—even her will to ask for God's mercy. He reached over and grasped the little book with its frayed black cover. With his fingertip, he lovingly traced the words "Holy Bible," their gilt lettering nearly rubbed away. He could at least pray for Susannah's inn, something he felt sure she would not do herself.

Grasping the Bible in his hands, he slumped forward, his elbows on his knees, his forehead pressed against the book's grainy cover. "Dear heavenly Father, I ask that You stop the rain and spare this inn from floodwaters. And please, Lord, give me the right words that I might convince the board to situate a depot here."

Unsure if it were seemly to ask the Lord for Susannah's affection, Thad's prayer faltered. He felt his lips twist in a wry grin. God knew the deepest secrets of his heart. "Dear Father, whether or not she could ever feel any measure of affection for me, just allow my actions to be a blessing to Susannah's life, and never again a trespass against it."

Thad winced as the dagger of remorse jabbed at his heart. To love the widow of a man he sent to die seemed somehow repugnant and perhaps evil. He couldn't deny that he had admired Susannah's picture George had shown him weeks before he sent George on that fateful mission. Had the haunting image of the lovely Susannah played a part in his choosing George to lead that mission?

Thad shook his head. He didn't want to think that. In his heart, he knew Sergeant George Killion had been the best choice to lead the reconnaissance mission. But with his affection for Susannah Killion growing daily, he couldn't help drawing parallels with the story of King David, Bathsheba, and Uriah.

He shoved the troublesome thought back into the dark corner of his mind from where it had crept. "Dear Father, just help me to save Susannah's inn."

Thad raised his head and rested the Bible on his lap. He stuck his thumb into the pages and allowed the book to fall open randomly. His gaze lit on the last two verses of the eighty-fourth Psalm. *"For the Lord God is a sun and shield: the Lord will give grace and glory: no good thing will he withhold from them that walk uprightly. O Lord of hosts, blessed is the man that trusteth in thee."*

Thad read the scripture over twice. When he closed the Bible and set it back on the table, he noticed the thunder had ceased and the room had lightened. His gaze traveled to the floorboards in the center of the room. There, morning sunlight pooled from a bright shaft slanting between the dark curtains. The rain had stopped.

A soft rap at his door pulled him up from the bed. He opened the door to find Lilly holding a steaming pitcher of water.

"I'm sorry for being so tardy with your shaving water, Captain Sutton." She hurried past him into the room, clean towels draped over her arm. "The inn is full of travelers and every one of them out of sorts, it seems."

"It's quite all right, Lilly. The weather would have delayed me anyway." Smiling, he took the pitcher of hot water from her frail-looking hands. Despite her slight build, Thad had found young Lilly Macklin to be a bundle of energy when it came to keeping up the rooms. Georgiana had explained in her childish innocence that "Lilly has to live here now, 'cause her papa was mean to her."

Not only was Thad glad that Lilly had a safer environment, but he was also happy that some of the workload had been shifted from Susannah's shoulders.

Lilly carefully laid the towels on the washstand. "Is there anything else you require, Captain Sutton?"

"I was wondering if you knew whether or not Ruben might have time today to help me with a project?"

She blushed prettily, causing Thad's smile to widen. He'd seen the two young people holding hands at the church social and determined they were sweethearts. "Captain Heywood's drivers see to his mules, and another stage is not due till Friday, so I don't see why he wouldn't."

After Lilly left the room, Thad quickly shaved, scraping off his stubble of beard with impatient strokes of his razor. He scooped handfuls of hot water from the washbowl and splashed his face, wincing when it stung the place on his chin he'd nicked in his hurry. He wiped the towel over his face. Glimpsing his reflection in the washstand mirror, he dabbed at the drops of blood oozing from the cleft of his chin.

No time to fuss with shaving cuts or linger over breakfast in the dining room. He might grab a cup of coffee and one of Susannah's biscuits, but he couldn't afford to waste one minute of daylight.

Thad glanced out the window. The pewter clouds had parted, showing widening patches of clear blue sky. A blue jay squawked and flew from the oak tree, sending a shower of rain droplets shimmering in the sunlight. God had answered his prayer, gifting him with a clear day. If he and Ruben could get a load of lumber down to the feeder dam, maybe—just maybe—they could shore up the canal walls enough to hold if the Whitewater River overflowed.

⁂

Susannah dropped dollops of dumpling dough into the large pot of bubbling chicken broth. Though it was the twenty-fourth of May, the past several evenings had been cool. After a day of working in chest-high canal water, Thad and Ruben would appreciate a hearty plate of chicken and dumplings.

She glanced through the open kitchen door. The sun sat like a red ball just above the little woods behind the inn. Soon it would slip behind the stand of trees. She hadn't seen Thad or her nephew since noon, when she'd hastily packed them a lunch basket.

For five days, they'd worked from dawn until dusk alongside a dozen or so of Promise's residents, reinforcing the canal walls. Each evening she'd watched Thad, covered in mud and sweat, lumber up to the inn's backyard pump.

Her admiration for Thad had grown daily. He had no vested interest in saving the canal—or the Killion House Inn. Yet he'd alerted the town council to the erosion he'd found in the canal walls. Too proud to admit they needed advice from a railroad man, the council had claimed they knew of the damage and had planned to address it—something Susannah doubted. Then, despite their contempt, Thad had worked shoulder-to-shoulder with the men of Promise to shore up the canal walls.

"Mmm, tell me that's chicken and dumplings."

Susannah whirled around at Thad's voice, feeling as if her thoughts had caused him to materialize. "Yes. Yes, it is." She wished she could rein in her galloping heart that sent heat surging to her face.

Thad stepped into the kitchen and inhaled deeply. His shirtsleeves were rolled above his elbows and droplets of well water sparkled on his dark curls. The late afternoon sun streaming through the open kitchen door wreathed his chiseled features in a golden aura.

The sight snatched Susannah's breath away.

Flustered, she turned her attention back to the dumplings, lifting the lid from the pot for a quick peek. Hopefully he'd attribute any extra color in her face to the steam spiraling from the bubbling pot. "Where's Ruben?"

"He's still washing up at the pump." Thad stepped nearer the stove to sniff the savory steam.

"Do you think the canal will hold?" Susannah kept her face averted from his, trying not to let her voice reveal her concern. Yesterday they'd gotten word that in the lowlands several miles north of Promise, the Whitewater River had breached its banks.

"It has a better chance of holding than before we began reinforcing the banks. But if it doesn't, Ruben and I have a wagon full of gunnysacks filled with sand to build a barrier between the basin and the inn."

He touched her shoulder, sending pleasant tingles through her body. "Susannah, you know I will do everything I can to protect this inn."

Susannah slid the pot of chicken and dumplings to the front corner of the cookstove farthest from the firebox. She reached up and gave the damper on the stovepipe a twist, half closing it, then turned toward Thad. The gratitude that had been simmering inside her all week bubbled to the surface, flooding her eyes. She gave his hand a quick squeeze while her lashes beat back the tears misting his features. "I want you to know that whatever happens, I—all of us here at the inn—appreciate your efforts."

A sweet smile tipped the corners of his mouth. He caught both her hands in his, giving her fingers a warm return squeeze.

The sound of multiple footsteps trouping down the stairs, accompanied by a jumble of muted, unintelligible voices, registered vaguely in Susannah's ears. At the moment, it didn't matter to her that the inn's guests were filing into the dining room. Thad's nearness filled all her senses, crowding out all other stimuli.

"I know you do," he replied barely above a whisper while his tender gaze embraced hers.

Gripped by a trancelike state, Susannah's eyelids closed and she leaned toward him. The next moment, she would be in his arms.

"Mamma, I can't find Dolly anywhere!" Georgiana's urgent whine yanked Susannah from the spell, and she jerked away from Thad, her face burning.

"Where is the last place you remember being with Dolly?" Thad had come around to kneel beside Georgiana. He brushed his thumb across her cheek, catching a tear.

Georgiana's little brow puckered. Thad's quiet voice seemed to have calmed her panicked tone. "We were having tea over by the mule stable with Captain Heywood's mules, Mac and Mol," she said with a sniff.

Susannah gasped. "Georgiana, that is much farther from the inn than you should go alone. And I've warned you about those mules. They could step on you!" Perhaps she'd depended too much lately on Lilly watching Georgiana.

"I wasn't alone, Mamma. Dolly was with me, and we stayed away from the mules' feet." Georgiana headed for the kitchen door. "I'm going to look for her."

Susannah started toward Georgiana. "No, you are not, young lady! It's nearly dark and we have a dining room full of guests waiting for supper." She glanced across the kitchen into the adjoining room. Through the doorway, she could see Lilly cutting bread at the sideboard while Naomi worked her way around the table pouring water into goblets.

Thad swung Georgiana up to his broad left shoulder. "Tell you what, moppet, I'll go look for Dolly first thing after supper, all right?"

Georgiana's head bobbed as Thad carried her to the dining room filling with guests.

A half hour after supper, Susannah absently lifted the last dripping plate from the dishpan and handed it to Naomi. She glanced toward the dark rectangle of the open kitchen door and felt her heart quiver.

Good to his word, Thad had left to look for Georgiana's doll the moment he'd finished eating. But he still hadn't returned, and Lilly had put Georgiana to bed still fussing for Dolly.

Susannah walked to the kitchen door and voiced the irrational concern squeezing her chest. "Captain Sutton's been gone a lot longer than it should take to walk to the mule stable and back."

It was unlike Thad to disappoint Georgiana. That thought filled Susannah with a warm glow. Yet she knew it wasn't just the kindness and affection he showed Georgiana or his daily toil to protect the inn that drew her heart to Thad Sutton like a sunflower following the sun's beam. That moment they'd shared just before Georgiana had walked into the kitchen this evening had wiped all doubt from Susannah's mind and heart. She cared for Thad Sutton like she'd never cared for any man since George.

Naomi dried a dish with a linen cloth and set it atop a stack of several others then cocked her head toward the kitchen door. "What on earth's got into those mules? They're just braying and carrying on like I've never heard! Maybe I should ask Ruben to go check." She deposited the plates in the cupboard, closed the doors, and twisted the wooden latch to fasten them.

"No, he's already gone to bed." Susannah smiled fondly. Earlier, she'd passed her nephew's bedroom, situated behind the dining room and between the storage room and linen closet. The poor boy was fast asleep. Susannah's heart swelled with pride for her brother's son. For days, he'd been working as hard as any grown man alongside Thad and the others repairing the canal walls.

"I expect Captain Sutton disturbed Mac and Mol's sleep looking for Georgiana's doll, but I'll go take a look." Susannah lifted the copper lantern from the iron hook beside the back door. She opened the lantern's glass door and lit the tallow candle from the sputtering flame of the lard-oil lamp on the kitchen table.

"Do you want me to go with you?" Stifling a yawn, Naomi removed her apron and hung it beside the washstand.

"No, just look in on Georgiana and go on to bed. I'm sure I won't get halfway to the stables before I meet Tha—Captain Sutton," Susannah amended, her cheeks tingling with warmth.

Naomi nodded and turned, but not quick enough to hide the knowing grin pushing up the corners of her mouth.

Outside, a chorus of chirping crickets and a honeysuckle-laced breeze welcomed Susannah to the late spring night. Naomi's smug look hadn't even bothered her. It would be useless to try to hide from her mother-in-law the fact that Thad Sutton lit her heart like the lantern in her hand lit the dew-laden grass at her feet.

As she neared the mule stable, she heard muffled voices and the sound of hurried footsteps retreating down the dirt towpath. Her heart sped with her feet. "Thad?"

Only a deep moan answered.

Lifting her lantern to direct its beam of light toward the sound, Susannah gasped, terror gripping her throat. Thad lay in a crumpled heap, his head resting in a pool of blood.

nine

Sure he'd heard his name being called, Thad tried to open his eyes. But when he managed to force his lids apart, a bright light sent shards of pain stabbing at his eyeballs. The unmistakable, sickly smell of blood assailed his nostrils.

Had he died? He thought he'd glimpsed the vision of an angel wreathed in a golden halo before the pain slammed his eyes shut. But there'd be no more pain in heaven. He'd read that in the Bible, hadn't he? *There shall be no more death, neither sorrow, nor crying, neither shall there be any more pain.* Yet his head throbbed like a fourteen-pound shot had been dropped on it. And someone was crying—no, sobbing.

Thad opened his mouth but could only push a groan through his lips.

"Thad! Thad, what happened?"

"Su—Susannah?" The effort to say her sweet name taxed his strength. Though fractured memories of the last several minutes began to assemble themselves in his scrambled brain, Thad had no energy to attempt to articulate them. He didn't want to move. He wanted simply to lie there, his head cradled in Susannah's soft lap.

But that wasn't what she was demanding of him. "Thad, you have to help me get you up. I can't lift you by myself."

When she gently lowered his head back to the ground, the sense of loss hurt Thad as much as the bands of searing pain rippling through his head.

She tugged on his arm, gasping between sobs with the exertion. "Dear Lord, help me get him to the inn, please. . . ."

An unexpected joy penetrated the dense fog threatening to swallow Thad's consciousness. Susannah had just called upon the Lord for help. *Lord, help us both.* He struggled to get onto all fours, but his limbs refused to obey.

"Susannah, what's happened?" Garrett Heywood's unmistakable voice intruded into the scrap of night Thad had shared with Susannah.

"Garrett, you've got to help me get him inside—" Sobs choked off Susannah's voice.

Surprised, and somewhat dismayed by the manner in which his prayer for help had been answered, Thad's body tensed as he bristled against accepting Heywood's help. Not only did he see the man as a rival for Susannah's affection, but Garrett Heywood could very well have been the assailant who'd bashed him in the head. He remembered a man's voice calling his name just before the night exploded in a shower of stars and the world went black.

"I heard Mac and Mol settin' up a commotion and thought I'd better see if a bobcat or some other critter was about." Heywood hoisted Thad to his feet and gave a low whistle. "Looks like somebody tried to take your head off, man."

Thad didn't even attempt to answer as Heywood, with Susannah's help, propelled him toward the inn. He fought for consciousness just so he could continue to feel Susannah's arm around him and her soft cheek against his.

Inside the inn, the lantern swinging in Heywood's hand set apparition-like shadows dancing around a little room. The earthy smells of wheat flour and coffee beans helped Thad recognize it as the inn's storeroom.

Susannah and Heywood lowered him to a rough pile of burlap sacks.

Thad struggled to stay awake. He wanted to find out who'd attacked him—and he didn't want to leave Susannah alone in the dark with Garrett Heywood. But as their faces blurred and the room dimmed, he had no choice but to surrender to the blackness closing over him.

ᨠ

A feeling of warmth was Thad's first conscious sensation.

Peering through squinted eyelids, his little blue and white room came into focus. The warmth he'd felt was the morning sun streaming through the window.

Had he dreamed it all?

He pushed against the feather mattress and tried to sit up, but the intense throbbing in his head caused him to sink back onto the pillow. It felt as if a couple of burly steel drivers wielding ten-pound hammers were driving railroad spikes into his head.

He groaned and touched his forehead. His fingertips found a smooth, cool band of cloth that told him it had not all been a bad dream. Someone had tried to kill him.

The door to his room creaked, snapping him to attention. Puzzled, he saw no one until his gaze slid down the doorjamb. It lit on a tumble of blond curls.

Georgiana crept in with an uncharacteristically somber look on her cherubic face.

Thad managed to rise up on one elbow and force a smile. "Hi there, moppet." His mind raced, trying to think of a gentle way to tell her what he'd found just before he'd been whacked. The memory of her beloved Dolly lying in the dirt with its china head smashed made his stomach go queasy.

She wandered over to his bed, and her little fingers picked at the patchwork quilt draped down the side of the mattress. "I'm sorry your head got bwoke, Tad. Dolly's head got bwoke, too." Her blue eyes shimmered for a moment before sending large teardrops sliding down her cheeks. The trauma seemed to have set back the progress the child had been making in her enunciation.

Thad's heart rent. "I'm sorry about that, moppet. I truly am." He reached down and caressed her baby-soft curls. He couldn't love this child more if she were his own daughter.

"Does your head hurt?" Georgiana unceremoniously climbed onto the edge of the mattress and crawled over the quilt to gently touch his bandaged head.

"Yeah, some," he lied as the steel drivers continued to slam their hammers down.

"I'm glad you didn't die. Dolly died." She sat cross-legged beside him, fresh tears sketching down her little face.

"I know, moppet." Thad reached over and with his fingertips wiped the moisture from her petal-soft, baby-plump cheeks. Her next comment froze his fingers there for a long moment.

"My Papa died. Mamma said you were with him. Did his head get bwoke?"

At Georgiana's innocent question, the awful scenes from the Battle of Buena Vista came thundering across the forefront of Thad's mind. "No, Georgiana, your papa's head didn't get broke." How much did she know? How much should a four-year-old be told of such things? While he pondered these questions, Georgiana moved on to a new question.

"Did they put Papa in a box? Gwamma said when Gwampa died they buwied him in a box."

"Yes, they did." Thad decided the best way to respond to her simple questions was with simple answers.

"Why?"

"Why do they bury people in boxes?" Thad realized that Georgiana, having never known her father, was simply exercising her childish curiosity. "Well. . ." He rubbed his thumb across a day's worth of stubble on his chin as he contemplated how to answer in terms Georgiana could understand. "The box is called a casket, and burying people we love in them is a way of showing respect."

"Wespec?"

"Respect." Thad couldn't help grinning. He'd never thought of himself as a teacher—except maybe of raw recruits. "It means we think well of someone."

"Georgiana!" Susannah's sharp voice yanked both Thad's and Georgiana's attentions toward the doorway.

"I'm sorry, Captain Sutton. She knows better than to go into guests' rooms." Her face full of dismay, Susannah hurried to his bedside and set Georgiana on the floor.

Georgiana planted her little fists on her hips and wrinkled her brow in defiance. "He's not a guest. He's Tad!"

"Now, soldier, we can't have any insubordination," Thad chided. But Georgiana's puzzled look destroyed his stern demeanor, tugging his mouth into a grin. "You have to mind your mamma," he explained then turned to her mother. "Georgiana was just expressing her concern for my head, and I was extending my condolences—in regards to Dolly."

Susannah gave her daughter a sharp pat on the bottom. "You go on downstairs and help Lilly dust the lobby—and stay out of the guests' rooms."

Georgiana lingered in the doorway. "I hope your head gets better, Tad."

Thad smiled as his heart melted. "Thanks, moppet. I'll be up and giving you piggyback rides before you know it."

He watched the little girl scamper out and wished with all his heart he could stay in Promise. As his gaze slid to Georgiana's mother, the feeling intensified. But his spirit drooped. The reasons he could not stay were myriad.

Susannah's fingers worried the edges of her blue calico apron. "I'm sorry if Georgiana disturbed your rest." She seemed to study the pattern in the quilt covering him. "I'll see that she doesn't bother—"

"Please don't. Don't deny me the joy of her company—or yours." He reached over and clasped her hand in his. Thad had always found her hands compelling. Lovelier in form than those of many debutantes he'd known. Though not as soft as the idle hands of wealthier ladies, Susannah's hands, roughened by honest labor, were hands to which a man could trust his life. And his love.

Their gazes both drifted to the third finger of her left hand resting in his. The finger still adorned with George Killion's gold wedding band.

Guilt jabbed at Thad's heart, and he released her hand.

She lifted her gaze to the bandage wrapped around his head. "How does your head feel?" Her voice sounded flustered, and her cheeks turned a deeper shade of rose.

"Like a crew is laying rail inside it." His chuckle, which made his head pound harder, was rewarded by Susannah's smile. "How'd I get up here, anyway? Last I remember I was on a pile of gunnysacks in the storeroom."

"After you fainted, I insisted Garrett help me get you to your room."

"Garrett, huh?" Thad heard his voice harden as a streak of jealousy slithered through him.

Her chin lifted a notch, and her voice sharpened. "Captain Heywood wasn't the one who attacked you, if that's what you're thinking." She glanced toward the window. "As you've well noticed, you're about as welcome in this town as a skunk at a picnic. The men who attacked you are cowards, but I'm sorry to say Promise has its share."

"Men?" Thad's interest piqued. He'd imagined his attacker had been a lone assailant. How could Susannah know it had been more than one man unless she'd seen the attack?

"When I went looking for you, I heard at least two men's voices and what sounded like more than one pair of boots running down the towpath. It was too dark to make out more than shapes. . .and when I saw you—" The catch in her voice sent Thad's repentant heart soaring.

Thad's sense of fairness convicted him. "I'm sorry I impugned Captain Heywood." The man *had* assisted him. The least he could do was to give Heywood the benefit of the doubt. An old worry crowded out thoughts of who might have cracked his head open. "Has the water level in the canal receded or is it rising?"

Susannah's face clouded. "It's at least six inches higher today than it was yesterday."

Thad pushed the quilt to his waist and tried to scoot to the edge of the bed. "Ruben and I need to sandbag the curve of the basin nearest the inn." He swung his bare leg over the edge of the bed, then realizing he was in his nightshirt, quickly pulled his leg back under the covers. Heat rushed from his neck to his bandaged hairline. He felt his eyes grow wide as he looked aghast at Susannah.

Her soft giggle did nothing to relieve his unease but her following comment helped. "Gar—Captain Heywood prepared you for bed."

He strove to restore some dignity to his voice. "I must ask you to leave so I can get dressed. We may have one more day before the floodwaters reach Promise."

She bent over him and gently grasped his shoulders, sending the pleasant scents of lye soap and rosewater cascading to his nostrils as she eased him back against the pillows. "You are going nowhere until your head is healed."

Their faces were only inches apart when their gazes locked and a sweet understanding seemed to pass between them. Then Susannah jerked away, breaking the connection as if she'd suddenly realized she was in a man's bedchamber.

A series of looks Thad could not entirely define registered on her beet red features before she turned toward the door. "I–I'll send Lilly up with a breakfast tray," she mumbled over her shoulder before making a hasty retreat.

Thad heaved a deep sigh and fell back onto the two feather pillows. She cared for him—deeply—as he cared for her. He'd seen it in her eyes. But the knowledge that his feelings for Susannah Killion were reciprocated did not erase the mountain of obstacles blocking any hope of a relationship between them.

In that brief moment of understanding—of connection— what emotions had he seen flash across her face? Surprise? Of course. Fear? A touch. Longing? Without a doubt. But it was the look of immense sadness he'd seen in her hazel eyes that continued to slash at his heart. She, too, saw the hopelessness of such a relationship. And now, this attack on him made it clear to Thad that for Susannah to be tied to him could make her, at best, a pariah in Promise or, at worst, put her in danger.

He rubbed the temples of his throbbing head and sent a desperate prayer winging heavenward from his heart. *Oh, Lord, I love them so much. There must be a way for Susannah and I to make this work—find a future together. Please show me a way. Just give me some hope. . . .*

ten

Hope. That's what it was.

An hour before supper, Susannah stepped out of the kitchen door with a bucket full of potato peelings. For the past several days, she'd attempted to define the feeling that caused her heart to float like the gossamer-winged butterflies flitting around the honeysuckle bush beside the stone steps.

She flung the bucket of peelings toward the ever-present greedy gaggle of geese, knowing something important had changed inside her. And it had happened the morning after Thad's assault.

That moment in his room when their gazes locked, something was planted in her heart that had not grown there for a very long time.

Hope.

Hope that she might actually be able to love again—to contemplate a life beyond widowhood. She longed to wrap her fingers around this blossoming hope, hold it to her heart, and breathe in the sweet fragrance of its promise. But she couldn't.

Her shoulders sagged as her heart deflated. He couldn't stay. Someone had tried to kill him. Or at least strongly encourage him to leave Promise. He could no more fit into her world than she could fit into his.

She gazed at the canal water still a good foot below the bank. Despite her best attempts to convince him to take a few more days of bed rest, thirty-six hours after his injury, Thad had returned to helping Ruben reinforce the canal.

This morning at breakfast, Naomi offered a prayer of thanks that the waters had lowered a bit. Following the prayer, she'd read from the Gospel of Matthew. *"Ask, and it shall be*

*given you; seek, and ye shall find; knock, and it shall be opened
unto you: For every one that asketh receiveth; and he that seeketh
findeth; and to him that knocketh it shall be opened."*

The words of the scripture had filled Susannah with bitter
bile. In the past several years, it seemed God had delighted in
slamming the door in her face while bellowing a resounding "No!"

And now He cruelly presented her with the hope of a new
love, yet sent it in the person of a man whose very purpose
here opposed her own.

&

Hours later Susannah tossed on her feather bed, her rolling
mind keeping sleep at bay. Dim moonlight streaming into
the room cast soft shadows on the papered walls. Undulating
leaves on the maple tree outside her window stroked the room
with shadowy fingers.

She pushed aside the quilt and swung her bare feet to the
smooth, cool surface of the wood floor.

Rounding the trundle bed, she smiled at the small quilt-
covered mound. Georgiana lay fast asleep, a peaceful look on
her angelic features. The sight of her daughter's blond curls
framing her face pinched Susannah's heart. The child looked
as much like her father as a four-year-old girl possibly could.

At the dresser, Susannah touched the top drawer's round
knob. She pulled the drawer open, and as she'd done countless
times during the past weeks, she lifted out George's last letter.
How could she feel free to give her heart to Thad—or to
anyone—when in so many ways, it remained tied to George?
Perhaps reading his final words might release her heart,
allowing it to move on.

With a resolute sigh, she pushed her thumbnail against the
sealing wax. But a series of quick raps on her bedroom door
stilled her hand, and she dropped the envelope back into the
drawer, unopened.

"Susannah!" The urgency in Thad's whispered voice propelled
her to the door.

What on earth could be the matter?

"Shh, you'll wake Georgiana," she warned in a rasped whisper as she opened the door a crack.

"I'm sorry to wake you, but I thought you should know, the canal has breached its banks. The water's just a couple yards from the inn's back door."

Fear slithered through her. Last year when floodwaters had gotten into the inn, she'd had to beg the banker for an additional loan to make repairs. It was doubtful the bank would extend her further credit. Even if she did somehow manage to secure the necessary funds, she would not be able to repay.

Susannah hurriedly dressed, knocked on the door to the adjoining room shared by Naomi and Lilly, and alerted them to the threat. A drowsy Lilly agreed to sleep in Susannah's bed so she could attend to Georgiana. Naomi insisted on accompanying Susannah downstairs.

"Lord, help us." The whispered prayer puffed from Naomi's lips as the two stood at the open kitchen door.

Dread knotted inside Susannah. A few minutes ago, Thad had said the water was a couple yards from the inn. But in the circle of light cast by the lamp he held aloft, she could see that the floodwaters had crept even closer and now covered the bottom step beneath the kitchen door.

"I'll go get Ruben," Naomi said as she turned and disappeared into the dark kitchen.

A few minutes later, Susannah and Naomi huddled together in the kitchen doorway, watching Thad and Ruben wade into the knee-deep water.

Susannah turned to Naomi. "We're going to have to make a barricade with the sandbags Thad and Ruben stockpiled. You might as well go back to bed."

"You know I won't sleep, daughter, but I can do something. I can pray." Naomi gave Susannah a quick hug. "It will be all right, daughter," she murmured before slipping back into the kitchen.

Susannah longed to possess Naomi's stubborn surety that everything would be all right. Hot tears prickled the back of her throat. At least, unlike Naomi, she could physically fight against the threat.

Soft, sandy mud squished between her bare toes as she stepped down into the floodwaters. It would just feel good to do something—anything.

"What do you think you're doing?" Thad's voice held a hard edge in the darkness.

She turned toward him, blinking against the light from his lantern. "This is my inn, and I'm going to help protect it from the flood, Captain Sutton."

His soft chuckle should have infuriated her, but it didn't. Instead, it sent ripples of joy surging ridiculously through her. He hung the lantern on one of the oak tree's lower limbs. His voice turned soft—concerned but not condescending. "I'm not sure you're strong enough to lug twenty-pound bags of sand."

"I've lugged around a fussy thirty-five-pound child on my hip while doing any number of chores at the same time," she told him in a dry tone.

"Excellent point!" His laugh blended with the summer night sounds of chirping crickets and croaking frogs, but the surrender in his voice was edged with admiration.

The rumbling of a wagon turned their attention to Ruben, who led their black gelding, Raven, hitched to the wagon full of sandbags.

"Don't come any closer, Ruben."

Thad's warning caused a new fear to spring up inside Susannah. In this darkness, it would be hard to tell flooded ground from the canal basin. If the horse or wagon fell into the canal, it could be disastrous.

Thad climbed to the back of the wagon and lifted down bags of sand to Ruben and Susannah. For the next three hours, they worked with little talk, only the occasional grunt as they passed the sandbags from one to the other.

At some point, Susannah realized it had started raining. Although she was used to physical work, her arms and back soon tired from the exertion. The rain plastered her hair to her face and her wet skirts clung to her legs until she could hardly move in the knee-deep water. She began to hope they would soon run out of sandbags.

Just when she thought she might collapse, Thad called out, "Well, reckon that will have to do."

Ruben went to unhitch the horse and wagon while Susannah and Thad gazed at the wall of sandbags about three-foot tall and twenty-foot long edging the canal basin in a crude semicircle.

Would it be enough? Susannah could only hope.

"Now all we can do is pray and see what the morning will bring." Thad's deep sigh held a weary resignation.

Susannah had no comment, allowing the croaking of the bullfrogs to fill the dark silence between them. Let Thad pray. Let Naomi pray. Susannah's prayers never seemed to reach beyond the treetops. Or if they did, God must turn a deaf ear to them. No, she would waste no more effort sending up prayers that would never be answered.

"Won't you pray with me, Susannah?" His soft entreaty gripped her with a sweet sadness.

The temptation to accept his invitation was strong, but she resisted it. If she didn't ask, she couldn't be rejected. "I—I don't think God listens to me."

Thad took her hand, sending tingles up her arm. "He listens, Susannah, and He answers. Sometimes He doesn't answer the way we want, but He always answers the way we need."

She pulled her fingers from his grasp. "Then tell Him I need my inn."

Afraid the lamplight might reveal the tears streaming down her face, Susannah turned away. Slogging through the water, she climbed the stone steps to the kitchen.

Up in her bedroom, she took off her drenched clothes,

moving quietly in the darkness so as not to wake Georgiana or Lilly. She cleaned up the best she could at the washstand then wiped the linen towel over her wet skin and hair before slipping into her nightdress.

Every muscle in her body ached as she climbed into bed beside Lilly. In less than four hours, it would be dawn. Though she was exhausted, worries about whether they'd have a useable inn in the morning made sleep seem improbable. Like Thad had said, all they could do was to wait and see.

She rubbed her hands, stiff from the work with the sandbags. A vague sense that something wasn't right niggled in her tired brain.

Suddenly, she felt the naked third finger of her left hand and gasped as the realization struck. Her wedding ring was gone. The likelihood of finding it in the mud was remote. It might have even fallen into the canal. Perhaps when the water receded she could look for it. . . .

An acute sadness engulfed her, and hot tears streamed from her eyes to her ears. She closed her eyes and tried to focus on George's image. It flickered for an instant, but the smiling face she saw as she drifted off to sleep belonged to Thad Sutton.

eleven

Susannah poured sugar over a bowl full of tart cherries and glanced out the kitchen door. The sandbag dike she'd helped Thad and Ruben construct had kept the floodwaters at bay. In the week since they'd built it, the barrier had instilled in her a measure of security.

For now, the water level remained stable. However, they'd heard an aqueduct and two locks had been damaged between Cincinnati and Promise. No canal boats had made it to Promise in a week. But at least the road hadn't been washed out, and a stage was due within the hour.

She ladled the cherries into waiting pans of dough, capped them with more dough, crimped the edges, and then used a paring knife to prick a wheat design in the top of each pie to vent. As she slid the pies in the oven, Susannah knew she wasn't making them for the stagecoach travelers. She'd planned the dessert with Thad Sutton in mind.

In fact, Captain Thad Sutton was never far from her mind. Each Sunday he was in Promise he squired her, Naomi, and Georgiana to church. He'd labored to protect the inn from a flood as if the place were his own. He obviously adored Georgiana, allowing her to follow him like a happy puppy. Since his arrival two months ago, Thad had become part of Promise, part of the Killion House Inn—part of Susannah's life.

But in recent days, he'd seemed withdrawn. She sensed his work here might be coming to a close. A melancholy wave rolled through her. She had warned Georgiana of becoming attached to the handsome captain, yet Susannah realized she, too, had succumbed to his charms.

"Have you seen young Ruben?"

The sound of Thad's voice from the threshold between the kitchen and hall set Susannah's heart bouncing. She turned from cleaning the worktable of flour and dough scraps. "No, come to think of it, I haven't seen him since breakfast. A stage is due in soon, so he's probably in the carriage house."

When Thad stepped into the kitchen, the frown on his face and the way his gaze avoided hers troubled Susannah.

"I—I'll be leaving for Indianapolis in a couple of days." Now, he looked directly into her eyes. "I want you to know that I'm going to do all in my power to convince my father and the other members of the railroad's board to situate a depot in Promise."

"I appreciate that—we all do." *Two days. In two days, he'll be gone.* The realization that Thad Sutton would be leaving her life filled Susannah with a crushing sadness.

"Ruben shows a real aptitude for surveying. I wanted to ask him if he'd be interested in learning the trade. He could begin as soon as I return from Indianapolis."

"Return? Your work is not finished here?" She went back to scraping flour and dough into a pie tin, hoping the happiness exploding inside her didn't register on her face.

"Yes, the preliminary work is done, but if the board is satisfied with my findings, there will be more work to do." He walked closer. "Are you glad, Susannah?" His soft voice had grown husky.

"Of course. I mean, Georgiana will be happy to hear it." Why did he have to stand so near? In another moment, the rockets igniting giddily inside her would propel her into his arms.

He reached out and touched her temple, gently turning her face toward his. "I'm glad Georgiana will be happy. But how do *you* feel about it, Susannah?"

She tilted her face, allowing it to press against his palm. How could she explain how she felt? In the space of one minute, he'd sent her to the pit of sadness and then shot her to the mountaintop of joy. Dizzy, that's how she felt. Dizzy with gladness. "I—I—"

"Mamma, I made pies, too." Georgiana stepped through the back door, covered in sandy mud, a dripping, grass-embedded, brownish-gray blob of the stuff in each hand.

Susannah rushed to her mud-caked child while Thad roared with laughter.

"Have you been digging in the garden again?" Susannah gently grasped her daughter by the shoulders. It was the only part of the little girl that didn't seem covered in dirt.

Georgiana nodded. "Lilly got Dolly's pieces so we could have a funeral for her. But Lilly had to go, so I had the funeral by myself." She held up the mud pies. "You and Gwamma make pies to take to funerals, so I made pies."

At her daughter's words, regret assailed Susannah. She remembered having promised Georgiana that they would have a funeral for the broken doll. But with Thad's injury and the floodwaters threatening the inn, she'd completely forgotten about it.

Thad's cheek dimpled with his grin. "Georgiana, that was a very nice thing you did for Dolly. And you have a couple of the best-looking pies I've ever seen." He knelt beside the little girl and examined her handiwork.

"Yes, but they need to be outside, baking in the sun." Susannah guided her daughter out of the kitchen door. After instructing her to place the "pies" on a flat stone near the back steps, she took Georgiana's mud-encrusted hand and led her to the pump.

Thad followed them from the kitchen and stopped at the pump to tousle Georgiana's mess of curls. "You two keep up the fine baking; I think I'll go to the carriage house and have that talk with Ruben."

"He's not there," Georgiana said, clapping her wet hands together and watching the droplets fly.

"Ruben's not in the carriage house?" Susannah turned to her daughter, whose expression suggested she relished knowing something adults didn't know.

"Do you know where he is?" Irritation skittered through Susannah. The stage would be along soon, and she needed Ruben to help the driver with the team.

"He went with Lilly 'cause her papa is angry," Georgiana supplied.

Susannah crouched down to get on eye-level with her daughter. "Did they go to Macklin's Sawmill?"

When Georgiana hunched her shoulders, dismay pushed a frustrated sigh from Susannah. She hated to ask Thad to help with the stage, but if Ruben didn't return in time, she'd have little choice. Susannah knew that one of the reasons stagecoach drivers were favorably disposed to stopping at Promise and the Killion House Inn instead of traveling on to the next town was because she provided them assistance with their teams.

"Don't concern yourself, Susannah. I'll see to the stagecoach if Ruben doesn't return in time," Thad offered as if he could read her thoughts.

Susannah rose. "Thank you." The words came out in a whoosh of relief.

"No trouble at all." He fixed her with a tender look that caused her pulse to quicken. "I'm glad I'm coming back, too," he intoned just above a whisper.

&

After checking on her pies and putting Georgiana down for a nap, Susannah decided to see if she could find Ruben and Lilly. Whatever problems Lilly had with her father, they could have at least let her or Naomi know they were leaving the inn. And when she found them, she planned to tell them just that, in no uncertain terms.

She stepped to the stairs where Papa Emil had fashioned a secret compartment for the cash box beneath the third riser.

If she had to leave the inn, she might as well stop by the gristmill and buy a bag of cornmeal.

But when she lifted the riser, her heart froze. The little space was empty. She lowered the board back in place and rushed to the desk. Maybe Naomi had moved the cash box for some reason. Praying that was the case, she peered into the dark interior of the desk's cubbyhole.

Nothing. All she could see was the extra supply of pens, ink, and register books. Frantically, she poked her hand into every pigeonhole shelf in the desk. No cash box.

Real fear shot through her. She needed that money to make the next note payment on the inn.

Hearing footsteps on the stairs, she stood and turned to see who it was.

Naomi, holding a piece of paper, her face as white as the sheet in her hand, stopped in her descent. She sank to the bottom step, allowing the paper to fall to the floor. Her narrow shoulders slumped as if all the strength had drained from her muscles. Her voice sounded hollow as she said, "They've gone—eloped it seems."

Ruben and Lilly must have taken the cash box. Fear, anger, and disappointment tangled in a painful wad in Susannah's belly. The bank had made it abundantly clear. Another late payment and Susannah must forfeit the inn.

Her mind raced, thinking of anyone who might be able and willing to loan her the money. There wasn't time to get word to her brother Frank in Hamilton County or her sister, Becky, or brother Jacob in Madison. Even if there were time, she hated to ask, especially since she'd been such a poor guardian to Ruben.

There was only one viable solution and everything in her rebelled against it. She'd have to ask Thad Sutton for a loan.

❧

Thad carried the last two buckets of water to fill the horse trough beside the inn. His heart felt as if it sparkled like the water in the early afternoon sun. He'd seen gladness in Susannah's eyes when he told her he would be returning to Promise.

His next thought tempered his joy. Perhaps it had not been gladness but hope that the board would not approve the railroad project after all. No. It was the news that he'd be returning that had lit her eyes. He was sure of it.

Why, he wondered, was he so afraid to believe his affection for Susannah was reciprocated?

George. George and the order Thad had given that ultimately resulted in George's death. Even if Susannah could get beyond the fact that Thad worked for the railroad—a railroad that threatened her inn every bit as much as the floods—she would one day have to learn about his involvement in George's death.

Thad's heart deflated just as the sharp blast from the coach driver's trumpet jerked his head up.

In a cloud of dust, the four matched sorrels brought the coach to a rattling stop in front of the inn.

Thad grabbed the bridle of one of the lead horses.

"Where's young Hale?" The coach creaked and swayed as the robust driver jumped to the ground with a jarring thud.

"I'm just filling in." Thad glanced up at the driver, who dragged his slouch hat off to swipe a red bandanna across his bald pate.

"Got to be back on the road in twenty minutes, so if you'd jist see to it that the horses each get a good drink then harness 'em back up, I'd be obliged." The driver cast the request over his shoulder as he opened the stagecoach door.

"Sure thing." Thad went about his work, paying little heed to the several passengers disembarking.

"Thaddeus Sutton, is that you?"

The vaguely familiar-sounding female voice yanked Thad's attention from the two horses sucking noisily at the trough. The reins slipped from his stunned fingers.

He found himself staring into the incredulous gaze of Olivia

Vanderpohl, daughter of Hirem Vanderpohl, vice president of the Union Railway Company. Her dark eyes twinkled with fun from the midst of her green bonnet as she smoothed her lace-gloved hand over the skirt of her traveling frock. The pale green-striped material reminded Thad of a gooseberry.

"Papa mentioned you were working in this area. But if the company is paying you so little you must do menial work to supplement your income, perhaps I should talk to him about giving you a raise."

Thad felt heat spread from his neck to his face. In the past year, he'd met the lovely debutante at several soirees. Something about her self-assured demeanor and the lift of her patrician nose always made him feel inferior. "I'm just doing a friend a favor," he managed.

One of the horses whinnied and shook his head, sending water droplets flying in all directions.

Thad grabbed the reins.

Olivia Vanderpohl took two steps backward. Giving an exasperated huff, she swiped at her skirt again. "I cannot wait for Papa to get the railroad built so I won't have to endure these barbaric stagecoach rides every time I visit Cincinnati!"

She turned to the middle-aged woman in black garb beside her. "Sadie, you go ahead and take the bags and sign us in. I'll be along directly."

Olivia's traveling companion gave a mute nod and headed to the inn's side door with two rather substantial-looking carpetbags.

Miss Vanderpohl's lips parted to show a glimpse of even, white teeth. "I'll have to tell Papa I found you hard at work, if somewhat unconventional work."

"I'll be traveling to Indianapolis myself in a couple of days to present my preliminary report to the board." Thad immediately regretted having divulged the information.

Olivia's face brightened. "How fortuitous! I'd planned to only stay overnight here, but perhaps I shall stay an extra day and we can travel on to Indianapolis together."

Thad's mind raced to find a reason not to share a stage-coach with Olivia Vanderpohl. "I had thought to travel by horseback."

Miss Vanderpohl's dark eyes sparked with apparent mischief as her voice affected a wounded tone. "Thaddeus Sutton, do you mean to tell me you'd prefer a sweaty old horse to me as a traveling companion?"

"No—no, of course not. . . ."

"Hey, man! I have four horses here that need water, not just two!" The driver's perturbed bellow as he unhitched the two remaining horses from the stagecoach saved Thad from any further explanation.

Olivia tapped Thad's forearm. "Wonderful! We'll travel together then. Well, I'll leave you to your. . .work," she said with a grin. "It's been ages since we last talked. The governor's ball, wasn't it?" She gave him a knowing look, her smile widening. "I look forward to catching up this evening at supper."

An uneasy feeling wriggled in the pit of Thad's stomach as he watched Olivia Vanderpohl walk through the inn's side door. He remembered well their conversations during the governor's ball last year. She'd flirted openly, leaving little doubt about her interest in him. Though she'd been one of the prettiest girls at the ball with her graceful, statuesque form, large dark eyes, and shiny chestnut hair, something about her had set his teeth on edge.

A worried frown dragged down the corners of Thad's mouth as he led the remaining two horses to the trough. A scorned Olivia Vanderpohl could be dangerous—not only to him, but to Promise and the Killion House Inn.

twelve

"May I have a word with you, Captain Sutton?" Susannah approached the lobby sitting area, struggling to keep the tremor from her voice. The presence of Miss Vanderpohl sitting beside Thad on the sofa did nothing to improve the state of Susannah's nerves.

Since her arrival yesterday afternoon, the daughter of the Union Railway Company's vice president had insisted on being treated like royalty. She'd demanded that her breakfast be brought to her room and complained about everything from the food to the bed linens. But Susannah realized what bothered her most about Olivia Vanderpohl was the attention she paid Thad Sutton.

"Yes, Susannah, of course." Thad sprung from the sofa, mumbling a quick apology to his seatmate.

The expression on Miss Vanderpohl's face could have been chiseled from ice.

Susannah led Thad to the kitchen. She dreaded the next few minutes worse than the time Elmer Gorbett, the local barber, had pulled two of her wisdom teeth.

"Susannah, what is it?" The kindness in Thad's voice and the way he took her hands in his nearly snatched away her nerve.

For a moment, Susannah entertained the idea of pretending she simply wanted his opinion of the supper menu. But to lose her courage now would mean she'd lose the inn to the bank. Instead, she took a deep breath and forced her gaze to meet his. "My cash box is missing—has been since yesterday, after Ruben and Lilly left."

"You think they took it?" A look of anger hardened his

features, and his gray eyes flashed like cold steel.

"What else can I think?" The tears she'd been determined to keep in check rolled unheeded down her face.

"Would you like for me to try to find them? Because I'd be glad to—"

"No." She shook her head. Ruben wasn't Thad's responsibility. "I—I need a loan—to make my note payment on the inn," she blurted, feeling her nerve slipping.

"Of course. How much do you need?"

"Forty dollars." Susannah cringed inside. It was a lot to ask, and she had no idea how she might repay it.

His sweet smile caressed her troubled heart, sending more tears sketching down her face. "The railroad has allowed me to set up an expense account at the bank here. I'm authorized to draw upon it for accommodations and other necessities." He gave her fingers a warm, comforting squeeze. "The Killion House Inn has simply requested an advance payment, that's all."

Susannah swallowed hard and looked down at the floor. If she kept gazing into his kind eyes, she'd fall into his arms and bawl like Georgiana. "I can't promise when I can repay you."

"No payment needed. Like I said, I'm simply making an advance payment against the time I plan to stay here. Now, don't fret another minute about it. I'll see to the business tomorrow." He bent and brushed a kiss across her forehead before striding back toward the lobby.

Touching her fingers to the skin still tingling from Thad's kiss, Susannah walked into the dark little pantry and pulled the door shut behind her. The emotional bubble that had grown inside her over the last twenty-four hours burst. She slid to the floor, hugged her knees against her chest, and sobbed.

The *click, click* of Naomi's quick, light steps on the kitchen floor filtered into Susannah's hiding place. The sound reminded Susannah that an inn full of patrons, including Thad and Miss Vanderpohl, would be expecting supper soon.

Rising, she sniffed, dried her eyes on her apron hem, and

reached for a jar of pickled beets on the dusty shelf above her. She couldn't afford the luxury of unbridled emotions.

With a jar of beets in each hand and her gumption bolstered, Susannah emerged from the pantry. This month's inn payment would be met. Beyond that, she would do as she'd done for the past four years—she'd take each day and each problem as it arose.

⚬

Four days later, Susannah lifted a newly washed pillowcase from the laundry basket. The roses embroidered on its hem told her it was from the room lately occupied by Olivia Vanderpohl.

Reminded of the woman who'd flirted so outrageously with Thad, Susannah snapped the fabric so hard it made a loud *crack*. She reached into her apron pocket for a wooden pin and rammed it down on the wet cloth she'd draped over the line.

If ever a woman had set her cap for a man, Olivia Vanderpohl had set hers for Thad Sutton! And the way he'd taken Olivia's elbow and assisted her into the stage then smiled as he followed her into the conveyance suggested he enjoyed her attentions.

Susannah welcomed the anger welling up inside her, flowing into her arms and exploding from her fingers. It helped to numb the hurt. Why had she been so silly to allow herself to become attached to Thad Sutton?

A match with Olivia Vanderpohl would secure Thad's position with the Union Railway Company and guarantee his advancement. And she'd gleaned from the conversations she'd overheard between him and Miss Vanderpohl that their fathers were the best of friends.

Jealousy gnawed at Susannah's belly. She flopped a wet sheet over the line and tugged out the wrinkles. Olivia Vanderpohl could offer Thad everything his heart might desire. All Susannah could offer beyond her ever-growing and abiding affection was a mortgaged inn—the very existence of which was threatened by the Union Railway Company.

Thad's departure seemed to have had as devastating an effect on Georgiana as it had on Susannah. The child had moped around since Thad left, even though he'd promised to bring her a surprise from Indianapolis.

A frown wrinkled Susannah's forehead when she glanced around the flapping sheet at her little girl. Georgiana sat listlessly on the bottom step beneath the kitchen door. The little rag doll Susannah had made for her to replace Dolly lay discarded at her feet.

Susannah's gaze drifted to the canal basin wharf from where Garrett Heywood's *Flying Eagle* had departed for Cincinnati a few hours earlier. A stab of guilt shot through her. Georgiana needed a father. Ever since the church social at the end of April, Garrett had faithfully attended Sunday worship services here in Promise. And she hadn't noticed so much as a hint of alcohol on his breath for months.

She pinned her spare day dress to the line, her heart sagging like the burdened twine. She shouldn't allow her own selfish feelings to deny Georgiana the benefit of a father figure in her life.

Besides, Thad could very well return from Indianapolis with news that he'd become affianced to Olivia Vanderpohl.

Thad.

There he was again. Always there. Always hovering—patrolling the boundaries of her consciousness. For years, she'd used the excuse of her undying love for George to cloister her heart away from any chance of further hurt.

She smiled, remembering the words of her brother Jacob when he officiated at her and George's wedding. *"The threefold cord of the husband, wife, and Lord is not easily broken."*

For years, she'd let her heart lay fallow, unwilling to allow the plowshare of a new relationship to crack its crusty surface. Yet Thad had slipped into her heart, planting something there she'd thought would never grow again. How could love. . . Yes, she'd call it what it was—love. How could love have bloomed in a heart kept so carefully uncultivated?

She looked over her shoulder at the meadow, and the answer nodded at her from myriad wildflowers. Her gaze flit like a butterfly over the expanse of yellow mustard plants, pinks, blue bachelor buttons, and snowy Queen Anne's lace. Only His hand that had planted this meadow could have planted the feeling growing inside her.

Another surge of anger shot through her, and she snapped a pillowcase against the faded blue of the summer sky. God had done this to her. Did He enjoy allowing her to touch the promise of love, just to snatch it away so He could watch her mourn the loss?

God had taken George. Her home and livelihood remained in constant jeopardy. A new love—a new dream—had been allowed to grow, only to be ripped away, leaving a fresh wound on her heart.

What next, God? What will You take from me next?

"Susannah? Susannah, do you hear me?"

Naomi's voice jerked Susannah from her reverie, drawing her attention to the bottom step beneath the kitchen door.

"I said this child is burning up!" Naomi stood, holding Georgiana and pressing her free hand against her granddaughter's rosy cheeks and forehead.

Susannah dropped a wet tablecloth back into the laundry basket and raced to her daughter. Fear shot through her as she touched Georgiana's frighteningly hot skin. She took her baby into her arms and headed inside.

The child had gone as limp as her rag doll, and her eyes looked glassy.

No, God, no! You can't have her, too!

Naomi followed them into the kitchen. "I'll brew some catnip tea." Her calm tone belied the concern in her eyes.

Upstairs, Susannah struggled to keep her voice light as she tucked Georgiana into her trundle bed. "Do you want your rag doll?"

Georgiana rolled her head back and forth on her pillow. "No. I want Tad."

Her daughter's reply squeezed Susannah's heart.

Out of the mouth of babes.

Susannah realized that Garrett Heywood—or any other man—would never be able to replace the man both she and her daughter wanted in their lives.

"I know, darling," Susannah murmured as she caressed her child's feverish face. "Me, too."

thirteen

Atop the jostling stagecoach, Thad inhaled a lungful of fresh country air as he watched the Indiana countryside bounce along. At the last stop, he'd opted to ride on the leather seat just behind the driver.

Inside the coach, his traveling companions had consisted of the Cheathams, a family of six on their way to Pennsylvania. Mr. Cheatham kept the coach's interior filled with cigar smoke, which blended nauseatingly with his wife's overpowering perfume. Their children, two boys and two girls, bickered constantly, making Thad's heart long for sweet-tempered Georgiana.

In truth, Thad's heart had never left Promise. Every time he closed his eyes, he could see Susannah standing in front of the inn, watching him climb into the coach bound for Indianapolis. She'd waved and smiled, but her hazel eyes had seemed extra bright. . .with unshed tears? He liked to think so.

The journey to Indianapolis had been no more pleasant than this return trip to Promise. But at least now he could escape the torments of his fellow travelers. There had been no escaping Olivia Vanderpohl's constant, maddeningly trivial chatter.

He couldn't help comparing Olivia's whining about difficulties in planning a soiree with the quiet grace Susannah displayed daily as she ran her inn. Or Olivia's tiresome chatter about the latest fashion and social gossip compared with the stimulating, if somewhat confrontational, conversations he'd had with Susannah.

In Indianapolis, he'd found himself caught up in Olivia's whirlwind of social events. With his jaw tightly locked, he'd grimaced through her birthday ball.

He'd carefully—and, to his mind, artfully—evaded Olivia's none-too-subtle hints that a marriage proposal from him would nicely crown her birthday soiree. Thad had to smile, remembering how he'd even managed to parry his father's hints that he should seriously consider the benefits of a Sutton–Vanderpohl alliance.

A frown immediately dragged down his smile. All his careful maneuvering around the matrimonial pitfalls seemed to have bought Thad little goodwill in the Union Railway Company boardroom. Although the members seemed pleased with his work, as well as his preliminary findings, they adamantly opposed the idea of situating a depot in Promise.

Hirem Vanderpohl insisted that the depot that would serve the Wayne County stretch of track be placed a few miles south, at Connersville. Vanderpohl also opposed Thad's alternative suggestion of placing a freight depot at Connersville and a passenger depot at Promise.

Remembering the pointed look the man gave him, Thad wondered again if Vanderpohl's opposition wasn't in retaliation for Thad disappointing Olivia. The frown deepened, and his jaw clenched. Olivia Vanderpohl is disappointed, so Susannah Killion must pay with her inn. The whole idea sickened him.

Anger sizzled inside him, and he closed his eyes, seeking out his Lord for peace. He dragged his wide-brimmed felt hat from his head, allowing the cool breeze to drift through his hair, imagining it as the touch of God's own calming fingers.

Heavenly Father, help me break the unhappy news to Susannah. Give her peace, show her Your love, and somehow, Father, find a way to save her inn.

Thad opened his eyes and realized they were nearing Promise. To his right, he could see the little woods that stretched down behind the Killion House Inn. A wagon full of lumber, undoubtedly from Macklin's Sawmill, rolled past them on the road.

Sadness and guilt twined around his heart, cinching tight. Along with the Killions, this little town had become an important part of his life. Thad swallowed the lump of remorse that gathered in his throat. He'd failed Promise. And he'd failed Susannah.

He braced himself as the driver lifted his brass horn to his mouth and loudly trumpeted their arrival.

When the coach rumbled to a stop in front of the inn, Thad climbed down, taking extra care with his leather satchel. A smile pulled at his mouth. Perhaps Georgiana would have something to smile about anyway.

He strode through the inn's front door, his heart hammering with anticipation of seeing Susannah again. Instead, he found a somber-faced Naomi registering the rowdy family that had been his coachmates.

When the last of the Cheathams headed up the stairs, Thad hurried to Naomi. For a moment, relieved surprise relaxed the tense lines in her face.

"Naomi, what is the matter? Where is Susannah?" The questions tumbled from his lips as a mounting sense of concern gripped him.

"Oh, Captain Sutton, I'm so glad you've returned. It's Georgiana. She's been suffering with an awful case of ague for days now."

The tears welling in Naomi's eyes sent fear spiraling through Thad. "It will be all right, Naomi." Thad patted the woman's hand and then bounded up the stairs, two steps at a time, praying that God would make his words come true.

❦

The sound of the bedroom door creaking open jerked Susannah's head up from her arm. Her muscles rebelled as she sat straight up and pushed her stiff shoulders back. She'd fallen asleep sitting on the floor beside Georgiana's trundle bed.

Blinking away the sleep, she touched Georgiana's face. Worry deepened and a weary sigh heaved Susannah's torso.

Her child's skin still burned and her little chest barely rose with her shallow breaths.

The sound of footsteps crossing the threshold told her Naomi must be bringing fresh water to bathe Georgiana.

"Susannah."

At Thad's soft voice, Susannah scrambled to her feet, waves of emotion surging through her. "Thad, I—I. . ." The tears springing in her eyes breached her lids and slid unheeded down her face.

The next moment he had her in his arms, lifting her to her feet and whispering soothing hushes and comforting reassurances in her ear.

Susannah clung to him, savoring the blessed moment. Only now did she realize just how much she'd missed him, how much she needed his nearness.

"My dear, dearest, Susannah," he murmured then pressed a kiss on her forehead as if she were Georgiana. "How is she?"

With his strong, comforting arm around her waist, they walked together to Georgiana's low bed.

"She's still feverish, but the dreadful shivers have calmed."

She walked to the washstand and poured the last bit of water into the bowl. Taking the damp scrap of cloth draped over the bowl's rim, she rewet it in the tepid liquid. "Naomi should be bringing fresh water soon." Susannah glanced at her sleeping daughter and felt a strong maternal tug. She knelt and bathed Georgiana's face with the cloth.

"You think that is wise, bathing her face with the window open?" The concern in Thad's voice touched a deep place in Susannah's heart.

What a wonderful father he would be to Georgiana.

She hurriedly shooed the thought from her mind and focused again on her daughter. "You sound like Dr. Wiggins," she told him, her lips stretching into a smile. "But my brother-in-law is a fine physician in Madison, and he's successfully treated many fever patients with this method."

"You mentioned Dr. Wiggins. She's being attended by a physician, then?" Thad knelt beside Georgiana and brushed a golden ringlet from her forehead.

Georgiana's pale lashes curling against her rosy cheeks fluttered for a moment, and her rosebud mouth pursed. Her little face rolled against the palm of his hand.

Susannah marveled, struck with the notion that even in her child's sleep, she must sense Thad's presence. "Yes, Dr. Wiggins has been treating her with quinine. He promised to come by again tomorrow." A lump of fear gathered in her throat. She felt Thad's arm slide around her waist again to give her a quick, reassuring squeeze, and the gripping fear ebbed.

All through the afternoon and evening, Susannah, Naomi, and Thad took turns sitting with Georgiana. The inn still had to be run, meals had to be made, and guests needed to be tended. The loss of Lilly and Ruben's help had become even more acute. Thad's willingness to help with everything from attending to Georgiana to serving and helping clean up after supper made Susannah want to weep with relief.

Though Susannah had wanted to stay by her child's bedside through the night, Thad insisted that she and Naomi rest in Naomi's room while he kept watch over Georgiana.

But after a couple of hours of fitful sleep, Susannah woke in the middle of the night to the distant sound of hushed murmurings. Wondering if Georgiana had awakened, she quietly slid from Naomi's bed. Wrapping her voluminous dressing gown around her, she padded across the moon-drenched room to the door that opened to her and Georgiana's bedroom.

There, in the pale halo of a single taper, Thad knelt with his head bowed over Georgiana's bed, whispering prayers for her healing.

Susannah trod softly into his shadow that stretched across the floor, guilt smiting her conscience. Not once had she allowed her worried heart to prostrate itself before the throne of God on Georgiana's behalf.

"Tad. Mamma."

At the tiny voice, raspy with sleep, Susannah rushed to her daughter's bedside. Grabbing the low rail of the trundle bed, she sank to the floor beside Thad.

"We're here, darling. We're both here." She touched Georgiana's face, and relief surged through her. Though her child's skin still felt far warmer than Susannah would like, Georgiana's fever seemed to have cooled some.

Georgiana's hand went to her throat. "Mamma, my thwoat hurts." She scrunched up her face with a visibly painful swallow. "Gwamma and Tad pwayed for me," she rasped. "Why don't you pway for me? Don't you want my thwoat to get better?"

For so long, Susannah had allowed her anger at God to separate her from Him. Like a petulant child, she had turned her back and refused to speak to her Lord. Now God might take from her the most important thing in her life.

"Of course, my darling," she murmured through a broken sob. "Of course I will pray for you." And it was true. Suddenly, Susannah wanted to reconnect with her heavenly Father—to pray and beg the Almighty to spare her child—to find again the solace she had spurned for years.

A giant knot of panic balled up in her chest. She wasn't sure she even knew how to pray anymore. She turned helplessly to Thad and felt his arm tighten around her waist.

His gaze melted into hers as he pulled her against him, seeming to sense her silent plea for help. He turned a gentle smile toward her sick daughter. "Would it be all right if your Mamma and I pray together for you?"

Georgiana nodded.

Thad clasped Susannah's hand in his and prayed the words she couldn't say. "Oh, Father, we ask that You cover our precious Georgiana with Your healing hand and restore her health. And please, Father, open our hearts to Your endless love and strengthen our faith."

Naomi's constant prayers hadn't managed to dent Susannah's stubborn resistance. But here in the darkened room on her knees, the words of Thad's prayer pried open the door to her heart, so long barred shut. For the first time in years, Susannah felt the blessed light of God's love shine its warmth all the way to her soul.

"Please, God, please heal my baby. Please. . ." Joyful sobs swallowed her words as a sense of peace overwhelmed her. God had heard her. She knew it. She felt it. Whatever else might happen in her life, she knew she would never again attempt to sever the blessed cord that connected her soul with the Almighty.

For a long while, as Georgiana slept peacefully, Susannah sat on the floor and wept in Thad's arms. How wonderful to be rocked in his comforting embrace as sweet, blessed moments stretched into the night like their linked shadows that reached across the room and up the walls.

Susannah knew she belonged here—belonged in Thad Sutton's arms. But at length, she wiped the remnants of her tears against the soft cotton of his shirtfront and pushed away. Thad had slept even less than she or Naomi. "You've hardly slept at all. Go on to your room now and I'll watch over Georgiana." Pushing against his shoulders, she forced her stiff legs to lift her body up.

"I've done without sleep many a night on watch while in the Army," he whispered, his voice husky—with sleep, or something else?

He rose and stood beside her, his arms slipping around her waist. "Let me know immediately if there's any change."

Susannah nodded, afraid to trust her voice. Did he know what his nearness did to her? Did he feel it, too?

It happened so suddenly, she had no time to prepare, to think, or to respond. He bent his head and brushed a tender kiss on her lips. "Good night," he murmured in a breathless whisper and then slipped out the door into the hallway.

Susannah closed the door with a tiny *click* and trudged back to her daughter's bedside. Her heart sank with her body as she lowered herself again to the floor.

She licked her lips as a sweet ache burrowed deeper inside her. Did his kiss mean anything more than friendship? How could it? His life belonged in Indianapolis. She realized that since his return, Thad hadn't once mentioned what had transpired between him and the Union Railway Company's board of directors—or Olivia Vanderpohl.

fourteen

"Please Mamma, me and Miss Lacy want to go, too." Clutching the china doll Thad had brought her from Indianapolis, Georgiana followed Susannah to the kitchen door.

Torn, Susannah hesitated as she reached for her bonnet on the peg beside the door. Her daughter had been free of the fever for scarcely three days. Yet Susannah's heart was still so full of thanksgiving for Georgiana's recovery, she found it difficult to deny her daughter anything. She didn't even correct the child's grammar.

"I don't know, Georgiana. It's a long walk to the blackberry thicket, and you're just beginning to get your strength back. Besides, there are snakes and chiggers around those brambles."

"Actually, I think an outing might do Georgiana and Miss Lacy some good." As he entered the kitchen from the hallway, Thad's quiet voice caused Susannah's heart to do a somersault.

"I'm not afraid of snakes and chiggers and I'll bwi–brr–ing my own basket." A hopeful look shone from Georgiana's uptilted face.

Susannah's resistance melted with her heart, and her lips emitted a sigh of surrender. "All right, but I'd better bring along an old quilt in case you and Miss Lacy need to rest."

"Come with us, Tad!" Bouncing with excitement, Georgiana tugged at his shirtsleeve.

The same longing exhibited in Georgiana's childish petition surged through Susannah. But she'd decided that both she and her daughter had become far too attached to Thad Sutton. One day soon, he would leave for good. Better now to begin pulling away from this man they'd come to love.

"Georgiana, I—I'm sure Thad has work to do," Susannah said weakly.

"Not at all. Free as a bird today."

His broad smile sent Susannah's heart tumbling again.

"I love blackberries." He bent down and lifted Georgiana to his shoulders. "Your Mamma and I could pick from the middle canes while you pick from the ones higher up. And it would keep you away from the snakes and chiggers."

"I'll get that quilt," Susannah murmured amid Georgiana's gleeful giggles. She hurried from the kitchen, hoping her face didn't display the happiness pinging around inside her.

A few minutes later, the June sun beat down on them as the three traversed the meadow between the inn and the little woods. Susannah's berry basket on her right arm bounced against her hip while she carried the small quilt for Georgiana's pallet tucked beneath the crook of her left arm. She was glad she'd insisted Georgiana wear a bonnet, but she still worried the heat might cause a recurrence of the fever.

From atop her perch on Thad's shoulders, Georgiana pointed toward the east end of the little woods. "I can see it! The blackbewwies are over there."

Susannah marveled at the patience Thad showed with Georgiana. He never murmured a complaint as the little girl's berry basket, with the china doll nestled inside, bumped against his shoulder with each step. Instead, he kept a running conversation with his diminutive passenger about all the delectable desserts that could be made from blackberries.

A familiar pain raked at Susannah's heart. If only she could allow herself to believe there was a way for the three of them to make a family. *Oh, Lord, if there could just be some way for him to stay in Promise. . . .*

She smiled at the ease with which the prayer flitted from her heart. She looked at Thad's profile with her laughing daughter on his shoulders, his hands securely wrapped around Georgiana's tanned bare feet. Susannah's thankful tears blurred the image. She knew her reconnection with God was one of the greater blessings Thad had brought into her life. Somehow he'd been able to revive her faith, something no preacher's sermon or even her devout mother-in-law had been able to accomplish.

"Blackbewwies!"

With Georgiana's triumphant announcement, Susannah's nostrils caught the sweet fragrance of the berries on the summer breeze. She realized they had indeed reached the northeast edge of the woods and the blackberry thickets.

The rough-leafed, sprawling canes shone with the glossy, dark fruit. Little specks of pinkish-red dotted the brambles where berries had not yet ripened, and Susannah noticed several yellow-centered white blossoms that promised later berries.

She turned to Thad and grinned up at the perspiration beading on his forehead. "You may want to put Georgiana down now and rest your shoulders after that walk. Besides, you're likely to end up with blackberry juice matted in your hair."

He threw back his head and laughed as he swung Georgiana to the ground. "Believe me, during my two years in the Army, my hair saw much worse than blackberry juice!"

As they shared a laugh, his gaze twinkled into hers, setting her heart dancing. Disconcerted, Susannah turned away and busied herself with spreading the quilt in a shaded patch of grass.

Georgiana set Miss Lacy, named for her snowy lace-over-rose taffeta dress, on one corner of the quilt.

"Be careful not to get blackberry stains on Miss Lacy's dress," Susannah cautioned her daughter. "You know how hard it is to get those stains out." The doll was one of the finer ones Susannah had ever seen, and she knew it must have cost dearly.

Thad's fond smile swung from Miss Lacy to Georgiana. "Miss Lacy seemed so lonely on that store shelf. I knew she needed a little girl to love her more than she needed a dress that never got mussed."

Susannah blinked quickly, swallowing the knot of tears that had gathered in her throat. Every time she thought her affection for the man could not deepen, he proved her wrong. She'd seen the pained regret on his face several weeks ago when he'd been unable to save Georgiana's beloved Dolly. Susannah was glad that her daughter had attached herself so quickly to the new doll. Miss Lacy seemed to have helped heal the unhappy incident with Dolly for both Thad and Georgiana.

For about an hour, they worked around the brambles, plucking the plump, dark berries.

"Be careful of the thorns, moppet," Thad warned Georgiana, who once again sat astride his shoulders.

Susannah noticed his careful movements so as to keep a safe distance between Georgiana's face and the briars. She glanced up to see a big juicy berry slip from Georgiana's hand and plop onto Thad's forehead.

Thad just grinned and swiped at a sticky, dark rivulet trickling down his forehead.

"Can't say I didn't warn you." Susannah laughed and sent him a sideways grin, earning her a barrage of berries against the back of her bonnet.

At length, Georgiana, who'd most likely eaten more berries than she dropped into her little basket, yawned. "I'm sleepy." She rubbed her eyes with blackberry-stained fists.

Thad reached above his shoulder and took her basket, handing it to Susannah. "I think it's time for you and Miss Lacy to take a nap, moppet."

In one smooth motion, he lifted Georgiana from his shoulders and cradled her in his arms. He tenderly laid her on the quilt pallet, tucking Miss Lacy beside her.

After he returned to the blackberry brambles, several minutes of silence stretched between him and Susannah. An indefinable tension charged the atmosphere around them.

Compelled to break the uneasy silence, Susannah spoke

first. "Thank you for Georgiana's new doll." Did her voice sound too stilted? "I don't think I thanked you."

He sent her that devastating grin that had become so familiar to her. "The look in Georgiana's eyes when I handed it to her was plenty thanks for me."

"Did you have a pleasant trip to Indianapolis?" The harder she tried to sound casual, the more her voice tightened. She wasn't about to mention Olivia Vanderpohl but hoped in a roundabout way to glean some sense of his feelings for the woman.

"Pleasant enough, I suppose." His tone unreadable, he kept his gaze fixed on his hands, gingerly plucking berries from the thorny brambles.

Something in his evasive demeanor troubled Susannah. Did it have to do with the railroad, Miss Vanderpohl, or both?

After several more minutes of uneasy quiet, he set his basket down in the grass and then slowly straightened to face her. At last he sighed deeply and looked her directly in the eyes.

Susannah quaked inwardly as she watched serious lines draw his features taut.

"I'm sorry, Susannah. I wasn't able to convince the board to situate a passenger depot here."

The news should have hit her harder than it did. Instead, Susannah found herself wanting to relieve the look of remorse furrowing his brow.

"I know you did your best." She reached out and took his hand. "We still have the stagecoach traffic," she said, forcing a smile.

At a rustling of the grass near her feet, she glanced down in time to see a little green snake slither past the front hem of her skirt.

"Ahh!" she screeched. Startled more from the sudden movement than the harmless snake, she jumped in the opposite direction from which the reptile had headed.

The next instant, she found herself in Thad's embrace.

Flustered and ready to push away, she lifted her face, and their gazes locked.

His arms gently pulled her closer. And this time, there was no doubt what emotion she saw in his eyes.

Her heart slamming in her ears, Susannah closed her eyes as his mouth captured hers. She eagerly welcomed his kiss. For one blissful moment, the coming railroad, Olivia Vanderpohl—all of Susannah's questions and concerns—drifted away.

Too soon, he lifted his head and released her lips, leaving her with a forlorn yearning for the tender moment now past.

In the harsh light of day, reality came rushing back. This kiss was no surprise. She had allowed it—perhaps even invited it. Heat leaped to Susannah's face. As badly as she would like to believe she and Thad could have a future together, a mountain of immovable obstacles still stood in the way.

She pushed hard against his chest, twisting out of his embrace.

A confused, stricken look dulled his gray eyes. "Susannah, I—"

"Mamma! I'm thirsty!" Georgiana's sleepy voice broke in, saving Susannah from any further exchange.

Susannah hurried to her daughter's side. Helping Georgiana up, she took ridiculous pains to smooth wrinkles from the child's patched and faded dress. "It's time to head back so you can get a drink at the pump. We have enough berries for several pies, and Grandma will soon need us to help with dinner."

Although every word was the truth, Susannah knew the real reason she wanted to get back to the inn. She couldn't bear another moment alone with Thad.

She folded the quilt and gathered the baskets as Thad hoisted Georgiana to his shoulders. The kiss had shaken her to her core. She couldn't look at him. The embarrassment smoldering inside her like hot coals flamed into a quick anger. How could he have allowed something like that to happen when he knew they had no hope of a future together?

Susannah carefully kept her steps a pace or two behind his, discouraging any conversation. She trudged through the knee-high weeds, clutching the berry basket so hard her fingers cramped.

She should never have allowed him to come with her and Georgiana. She'd vowed to distance herself from him, and that was exactly what she must do. But the longer he remained in Promise and at the Killion House Inn, the harder that task would be.

Oh, Lord, if he cannot stay, please hurry and send him back to Indianapolis.

As they waded through the weeds, Susannah gazed at Thad Sutton's broad back and felt her resolve wither with her prayer.

fifteen

Thad Sutton slammed his pen on the desktop. He picked up the paper before him, wadded it into a crumpled ball, and pitched it among several of its fellows littering his bedroom floor.

Leaning back in his chair, he stretched his cramped shoulder muscles and pressed his fingertips against his throbbing temples. At last, he surrendered to the realization that securing both the Killion House Inn and his position with the Union Railway Company was an impossible fool's errand. His every attempt to accomplish both goals in a respectful, yet persuasive, letter to his father seemed woefully inadequate.

"Drivel! Idiotic drivel!" Thad's brain echoed with the imagined sound of his father's irate voice.

He gazed through the window in front of his desk and blew out a tired breath. Since the floodwaters had receded, a constant flow of travelers had brought prosperity back to Susannah's inn. And now because of Josiah Sutton's stubborn insistence that he control his son and bend Thad to his will, Susannah, Naomi, and little Georgiana might well face homelessness.

Susannah.

Her image, her smile, *her touch*, never left him. Sweet thoughts of her continually strolled along the edges of his mind. Thad closed his eyes as his tongue crept out to taste, again, the remembered kiss on his lips.

Lord, help me, but I love her so.

In war, he'd led countless charges against the enemy. Yet here he sat, shrinking from the thought of igniting his father's ire.

He loved Susannah and Georgiana. He loved them with all his heart. And now they needed a champion.

Renewed anger straightened Thad in his chair, and he squared his shoulders, his resolve stiffening with his back. He would not cower like a frightened boy when the livelihood of the woman he loved hung in the balance.

Determined to not falter, he slipped another sheet of paper from the stack on his desk and dipped the nib of his pen into the inkwell.

Dear Lord, give me the words that will soften my father's heart and save this town and this inn.

Laying aside all concerns about his position with both the railroad board and his father, Thad penned his petition with forceful strokes. He shared with his father his feelings for Susannah and begged Josiah to use his influence with the board and join him in calling for reconsideration of a depot in Promise.

A few minutes later, Thad crossed the National Road, purposefully striding toward the post office. Not for the first time, he felt frustration at the lack of a telegraph office in Promise. Having become used to the service in Indianapolis, to be forced to wait for a reply to a letter seemed excruciatingly slow and primitive. He'd observed that it was generally the coming of rail service that brought the telegraph to a community. But paradoxically, it was that very rail service that threatened the existence of this town.

He wiped away the trickle of sweat meandering down his forehead. It wasn't so much the mid-June sun that caused the outcropping of perspiration as it was the missive tucked in his coat pocket. If his father viewed his request as insubordination, he could lose his position as engineer and surveyor for the railroad. But he'd never be able to live with himself if he sat by mutely and allowed the railroad to doom the Killion House Inn.

Lost in his reverie, Thad climbed the two steps to the post office's porch. He looked up just in time to prevent a collision with Susannah, who appeared lost in her own thoughts.

"Whoa there!" The words puffed breathlessly from his lips as he caught her about the waist. Finding her unexpectedly in his arms set his heart bucking like a skittish colt.

"Oh, I'm sorry!" Susannah jerked back, her face suffusing a deep pink. "I'm afraid I wasn't paying attention."

"Not at all. It was my fault entirely." He had to force his lips into a smile. It hurt that she always seemed repelled by his touch. To cover his disappointment, he glanced at the open letter in her hand. "Not bad news I hope."

"No." Her faint voice sounded evasive as she hurriedly shoved the paper into her skirt pocket.

At the sound of heavy-booted steps, Thad glanced over his shoulder to see Mick Macklin storming toward them.

Red faced, the man fixed a narrowed glare on Susannah. "Susannah Killion, you'd better tell me right here and now where that whelp of a nephew of yours went off to with my Lilly!"

Thad stepped quickly between Macklin and Susannah. The sawmill owner already reeked of alcohol, and it was not yet midmorning. Thad wanted to thrash the man for the bruises he'd seen on Lilly's face. *If that reprobate so much as lays a hand on Susannah. . .*

Drawing himself up to his full height of six feet, he glared at Macklin. "Mrs. Killion has no idea where your daughter is."

"I wasn't talkin' to you, railroad man!" Macklin infused the last two words with scorn and then spat over the porch rail.

"Mr. Macklin, I have not seen Lilly or Ruben for over two weeks." Susannah stepped from behind Thad's shoulder. Her voice was calm and her face placid, but Thad caught a flicker of fear in her hazel eyes.

The man squinted, his bloodshot eyes nearly disappearing in his unshaven face. He stabbed the air in front of Susannah with a meaty finger. "But you know where they are, don't ya?"

Thad grasped the man's shoulder. Even if Susannah did know the couple's whereabouts, which he doubted, he knew she wouldn't be keen on sharing that information with Macklin. "I suggest you be on your way, Mr. Macklin. And any further business you might have with Mrs. Killion, you can bring to me."

Through mean slits, Mick Macklin's glower swung between Thad and Susannah. "So that's the way it is, is it?"

His sly grin and snort strained Thad's self-control. The impropriety suggested in the man's look sent waves of molten anger bubbling up inside Thad. Only consideration for Susannah kept Thad from pummeling the drunkard senseless right there in front of Promise's post office.

"As friend and commanding officer to the lady's late husband, it is my duty to protect her honor as well as her person," he ground through his clenched jaw. "Mrs. Killion has told you she's not seen your daughter, so unless you have other business with her, I must insist you be on your way." He took another step toward Macklin, who backed up, nearly falling down the porch steps.

"I'll go, but I ain't done with ya. Neither of ya!" Mick growled, grabbing the handrail to regain his balance. He shot them a parting glare over his shoulder before plopping another wad of spittle onto the dusty path.

Thad turned to Susannah, his protective instincts raging. "Perhaps I should walk you back to the inn. I wouldn't want Macklin to cause you any trouble."

She gave her head a dismissive shake, though her face looked pale and her smile a bit wobbly. "Thank you, Thad, but I've handled far worse than a drunken Mick Macklin."

"Are you sure?" Thad allowed his gaze to melt into her lovely green eyes. He didn't want to leave her alone. He didn't want to leave her at all. "If you wait just a few moments while I mail this letter—"

"No, I really need to be getting back." She gave an unconvincing little laugh. "I'm sure Mick is halfway to the mill by now and has probably forgotten the entire conversation."

Thad watched her cross the National Road and head toward the inn. Only when he felt confident that Macklin was nowhere in sight did he turn back to the post office.

He touched his coat breast and the letter crinkled beneath his fingers. Over the summer, his mission in Promise had changed. Thad couldn't help wondering if God's reason for sending him here had less to do with surveying for a railroad than providing Susannah with a champion. He liked the thought. *Oh, Lord, if You would just allow me to spend the rest of my life as Susannah's champion. . .*

❧

Susannah sank to the bench beneath the pin oak tree in the inn's side yard. Her heart still raced from her near collision with Thad Sutton. Heat suffused her face as she remembered how the joy of feeling his arms around her had swamped her momentary embarrassment.

The familiar warm longing rose in her heart only to be drowned by a cold wave of reality. Thad was the enemy. However they might feel about each other made little difference. Almost certainly, his business at the post office had to do with communicating with the coldhearted company that seemed determined to starve Promise to death.

Another thought stabbed more sharply at her heart. Perhaps all his correspondence was not business related. Susannah's mind quickly fled painful imaginings of Thad exchanging letters of affection with Miss Olivia Vanderpohl.

Her gaze shifted to her brother's surprising letter in her lap. A renewed sense of relief and astonishment rolled through her as she eyed, for the third time, her sibling's firm script:

Dear little sister,
*   I hope this finds you, your kinswoman, Naomi, and precious little daughter, Georgiana, well. I write to inform you that our nephew, Ruben, and his sweetheart, Lilly, arrived safely at the parsonage here in Madison Tuesday last.*

They insisted upon being married, and although I harbored grave reservations, my dear wife, Rosaleen, persuaded me to agree, and I reluctantly consented to perform the nuptials. The newlyweds are living with us at the parsonage. Ruben has procured employment at Riverfront Porkpacking here in Madison. Lilly is proving to be a wonderful help with our three little girls. With another baby on the way, Rosaleen considers her a true blessing.

Both Ruben and Lilly regret deeply that they were not able to inform you of their leaving Promise prior to the event. It seems that threats made by Lilly's father, a truly unsavory character by all accounts, prompted their departure. They feared should they linger the man might bring his wrath to bear upon not only themselves but you and the Killion House Inn. Together, our young kin beg your forgiveness and pardon for any grief their actions might have caused. Lilly is eager to pen you a personal note of contrition but asked me to predicate it with this explanatory missive, desiring I assure you they are safe and legally united in marriage, sanctified by our Lord Jesus Christ.

The remainder of the letter held only news of their sister, Becky, and her family and recent happenings at their church in Madison.

Praying God will keep you and yours always in His tender care,

Your humble servant and beloved brother,

Jacob Hale

Irritation prickled as Susannah read the salutation. She'd found no mention of the money with which the young couple had absconded.

While she considered how she might broach the subject to her brother in an answering letter, a quiet shadow fell across the pages in her hand.

"Susannah." The unexpected voice sounded troubled.

Susannah's attention jerked up to Esther Murdoch's distraught face. A normally cheerful person, the preacher's wife's grim expression filled Susannah with alarm.

"Yes, Esther, is something the matter?" A sense of dread caused Susannah's fingers to tremble as she slipped Jacob's letter back into the envelope and shoved it into her skirt pocket.

"It's Mr. Sutton, the railroad man." She held up her hand and shook her head. "I don't abide any kind of gossip, and for my part, it won't go any further than this. But since the man is staying at your inn, Ezekiel thought you should know." Her gaze skittered across the canal, and she laced her plump fingers together as if in prayerful petition. Her next words came out in a rush, suggesting her eagerness to be done with the distasteful errand. "Sheriff Lykins has arrested him for vandalism."

sixteen

"Vandalism?" Thad yanked his arm from Sheriff Lykins's grasp. "Are you mad, man?" His anger mounting, he turned on the boardwalk in front of the general store where he'd just bought penny candy for Georgiana and faced his accuser. He knew that the sheriff, like many people in Promise, did not hold him in high regard. But to trump up false charges against him was beyond the pale!

Lykins shook his head. "I'm sorry, Mr. Sutton, but charges have been made by two eyewitnesses. Said they watched you saw the wicket clean off the upstream gate at Connell's Lock."

"Who said they saw me do that?" Thad tried to keep his voice down and his temper in check. "I have a right to know who my accusers are." He'd always known the people here were not keen on him, but he would never have imagined anyone would stoop to such treachery.

Thad felt the pressure of Sheriff Lykins's hand against his back, urging him on toward the brick courthouse half a block from the post office.

"Mick Macklin and Art Granger claimed they saw you leavin' the lock with a saw in your hand," the sheriff told him as they walked.

Lykins showed no interest in Thad's protest or assertion that he had no access to a saw.

As they walked the narrow alley beside the courthouse, the situation became frighteningly clear. Thad remembered Macklin's thinly veiled threat less than an hour ago in front of the post office. He suspected Macklin had done the damage himself. Thad also knew that Art Granger was a generally drunken ne'er-do-well who worked for Macklin at the sawmill. A jug of whiskey would easily buy the man's allegiance.

Behind the courthouse, Lykins guided Thad toward the jail. The weathered gray clapboard building jutting out from the rear of the courthouse looked as cheerless as Thad felt. Fear tightened around his chest like an iron band. With Thad unable to protect her, Mick Macklin might very well attempt to do Susannah harm.

When they reached the jail's open door, Thad stopped and tried one last, desperate time to retain his freedom. He turned to the sheriff. "Listen, Macklin threatened both me and Susannah Killion earlier today. He's upset that she allowed his daughter, Lilly, to stay at the inn after he'd beaten the girl. He's trumped this up to get me out of the way. I'm afraid he may harm Mrs. Killion or her inn."

"Tell it to the circuit judge next week." The increased pressure of the sheriff's hand on his back forced Thad through the doorway and into one of the two iron-barred cells. Lykins clanged the cell door shut and rammed a large iron key into the lock.

Thad heard the lock's tumblers click as he paced the spartan six-by-five-feet space. He shoved his fingers through his hair, fear and frustration raging through him. What if Mick Macklin was this very minute threatening Susannah?

"Please, Sheriff Lykins. . ." Thad grasped the cell bars, unashamed of the imploring tone tightening his voice. "Please check on Susannah Killion—"

"Thad!" Susannah burst through the jailhouse door, cutting off Thad's words. "I couldn't believe it when Esther Murdoch told me you'd been arrested."

The tears glistening in her lovely green eyes sent Thad's heart soaring. They confirmed what her sweet kiss had conveyed in the blackberry thicket—she cared for him.

Relief washed over Thad. At least, for the moment, she was safe. Even in the midst of his predicament, Thad couldn't help grinning as Susannah turned her indignation like a lioness on Sheriff Lykins.

"Tom Lykins, you let Captain Sutton out of that cell this instant!"

Lykins scratched the back of his neck and looked more than a little uncomfortable. "Wish I could, but I had two eyewitnesses swear they saw Captain Sutton here saw the wicket off the gate on Connell's Lock."

"That doesn't even make good common sense!" Susannah's passionate argument caused Thad to seriously consider having her represent him before the circuit judge. "Why on earth would he trouble himself to do such a silly thing? Why, Cy Pittman has probably already installed a new wicket by now. If Thad wanted to do real damage, wouldn't he have set fire to the lock. . .or blown it up. . .or something like that?" Her wild gesturing and raised voice set Lykins back on his heels. "Besides, only a month ago, Thad helped reinforce the canal walls to keep them from crumbling when the floodwaters came."

Tom Lykins scrubbed his hand across his weary-looking face and sighed. "Listen, Susannah, it's not my job to try and figure out why somebody might or might not do mischief. Shoot, it ain't even my job to figure out if he did it. That's the circuit judge's job. Mick Macklin and Art Granger said they saw him do it, so I'm obliged to hold him here until Judge Hendershot gets here next week and tries the case."

"Mick Macklin and Art Granger?" Susannah actually snorted. "You would take the word of two of Promise's most notorious drunks over a surveyor and engineer for the Union Railway Company?"

"I told ya, I don't have a choice." With outstretched hands, Lykins gestured his helplessness.

"Surely there is bail." The hopeful lilt in Susannah's voice clawed at Thad's heart.

"Well," Sheriff Lykins drawled, scratching the back of his

neck again, "the judge'd have to set bail and the judge ain't here. Most likely, a forty-dollar fine for such mischief would prob'ly satisfy the court. If you can pay that and sign a voucher promising to be responsible in case he takes off 'fore the judge gets here..."

Thad could stand mute no longer. "I won't leave Promise, Sheriff Lykins. And if you will just let me out, I can get you the money for the fine. The Union Railway Company has set up an expense account for me at the bank." There was no way Thad was going to allow Susannah to use her own money for his fine.

The sheriff shook his head. "Sorry, I cain't let you out." He glanced at the clock on a shelf above his cluttered desk. "The missus oughta be gittin' dinner on the table about now, and I know better'n to keep her waitin'." He gave a little chuckle. "I'll bring you a plate of grub when I get back."

"That won't be necessary, Tom," Susannah said in a quiet voice. "I'll see to Captain Sutton's meals." The sweet look on her face as her gaze swung from the sheriff to Thad made his arms ache to hold her.

"Suit yourself." Tom Lykins hunched his shoulders, plucked the cell key from his desktop, and lumbered out the jailhouse door.

Susannah neared the cell bars, her eyes flashing green fire. "I'm so angry with this town I could just spit!"

"Probably better be careful." Thad couldn't help teasing. "Lykins might arrest you for that."

She sent him a withering glare, and for the first time, Thad was glad for the bars between them. "How can you make jokes when you're in this—this cage?" She pointed at his dreary little confines.

"I'm sorry." The words floated out on a small chortle he couldn't hold back. He wrapped his hands around her fingers gripping the black iron bars between them. An overwhelming urge to protect her swept through him. "Promise me you will be careful of Mick Macklin. If he comes anywhere near you or the inn, let the sheriff know."

"It's Mick Macklin who should be afraid of me," she snapped, making Thad almost believe her.

Grinning, Thad caressed her fingers, reveling in the feel of her soft hand against his. "Don't worry, this will all be sorted out soon. Just go to the bank and ask them to write up an authorization note to have forty dollars withdrawn from my expense account. Bring the note here and I'll sign it, and then the bank manager will give you the money for my fine."

Susannah nodded again, but her smile quivered slightly. "I'll bring your dinner along with the note from the bank," she promised, giving his fingers a quick, warm squeeze before she turned and hurried out through the jailhouse door.

Thad gazed at the retreating back of this beautiful, courageous woman and swallowed down the lump that had gathered in his throat. What an amazing helpmate she would be if only God would allow him to make her his forever.

Dear Lord, please protect her. Just protect her until I can get out of this place.

&

Her jaw clenched, Susannah wiped the tears streaming down her face as she stomped toward the bank. How petty and mean of Mick Macklin to have Thad arrested just to get back at her for helping Lilly. Although she was still disappointed at Ruben and Lilly for taking the inn's money, Susannah was thankful Ruben had taken Lilly away from that awful man.

Stopping before the three stone steps in front of the bank, Susannah took a deep breath. Though her relationship with Fergus McDougal, the bank manager, had been strained at times, she felt confident he would understand the situation and respect Thad's wishes.

Oh, Lord, please let Fergus allow me to do this on Thad's behalf.

With another deep breath, she mounted the steps and entered the brick building. In the large, high-ceilinged room, her footfalls echoed on the smooth wood floor. The smells of ink, paper, and leather assailed her nostrils. Three clerks wearing green eyeshades sat huddled together in one corner. They seemed oblivious to everything but the mounds of paper on their desks over which they bent, constantly scribbling.

Susannah always found the bank more than a little intimidating. Everything about it reminded her it was a man's domain. But this time, especially, she mustn't allow herself to be cowed by the place. Thad's freedom depended upon it.

She strode to a large mahogany table usually occupied by Mr. McDougal. Gleaming dust-free in the late morning sun spilling across its top, the desk displayed an exactly centered green felt blotter. Above the blotter, a half dozen inkwells holding black pens stood like military sentries. But the overstuffed brown leather chair behind the desk sat empty.

"Mrs. Killion, is there something I can do for you?"

Susannah jumped at Fergus McDougal's booming voice. Heat suffusing her face, she willed her heart to a slower canter.

"The payment on your note is not due for another two weeks." Sending her a congenial smile, he motioned for her to be seated in one of the two ladder-backed chairs flanking the desk.

After she'd situated herself on the chair's horsehair-upholstered seat, McDougal rounded the desk and lowered his rotund bulk to the giant padded desk chair. He lounged against the chair's cushy back, smoothed down his gray mustache, and emitted a long, contented sigh. Fergus McDougal always reminded Susannah of a plump Scottish terrier.

"It is not on my own behalf that I'm here today, Mr. McDougal." Straightening her back and squaring her shoulders, Susannah laced her fingers in her lap and strove to affect her most businesslike voice and demeanor. "I am here on behalf of one of the residents of the Killion House Inn. Captain Thaddeus Sutton of the Union Railway Company—"

McDougal waved a beefy hand and shook his head, his bushy gray eyebrows knitting together in a grim scowl. "On my way back from dinner, I heard that Sheriff Lykins has the scoundrel in jail for vandalism. It seems he can't wait for the railroad to bring an end to our canal."

Irritation marched up Susannah's spine, stiffening her back. She knew McDougal had helped to finance the canal project and only grudgingly did business with the Union Railway Company. His eagerness to believe Thad guilty irked her. She swallowed down the retort that clawed at her throat for its freedom. The worst thing she could do would be to offend Fergus McDougal.

She clasped her hands in her lap until they were nearly numb and tempered her voice. "Captain Sutton maintains his innocence in the matter and has asked me to request a withdrawal of forty dollars from his expense account."

McDougal shook his head. "The man would have to come in and sign for it, and since he's not in a position to do that, there's really nothing I can do."

"I will take the note to him and bring it back to you signed." Susannah hurriedly blurted the offer, anxious to clear away all impediments to acquiring the money that would free Thad.

Fergus McDougal gave her a condescending, almost pitying smile. "I know you are not used to doing business beyond your little inn, but I would really need to witness the signature."

"You wouldn't trust me or Sheriff Lykins to witness the signing?" Susannah didn't even try to keep the contempt from her voice.

The banker's round face turned a deeper shade of pink, and he cleared his throat. He looked toward the trio of clerks and crooked his finger. "Boswell!"

A few spindly legged strides brought the summoned clerk to McDougal's desk.

"Boswell, bring me Mr. Sutton's file, please."

The young clerk murmured his acquiescence and left for

his cluttered corner. After a few tense moments of silence, he returned and placed several papers on the bank manager's desk.

McDougal perused the papers and, following a series of muted harrumphs, looked up at Susannah. "I'm afraid it is just as I recalled. Mr. Sutton has drawn within ten dollars of the account's limit until the Union Railway Company refreshes the account with a new infusion of capital." He looked at Susannah as if he were addressing a slow child. "There is not forty dollars in the account. Only ten."

Fear warred with fury inside Susannah. Was Fergus McDougal telling the truth, or did he want to keep Thad in jail for spite? She had no idea but wished she could slap the smug grin off the bank manager's fleshy face. Instead, she thanked him for his time and left the bank before she said something she might later regret.

Dear Lord, why does life have to be so unfair?

The late June breeze dried her tears as she headed for the inn. Hadn't she learned to not rail at God? Thad himself would tell her to only trust. Life was what it was.

But she had no time to ponder such weighty questions. Right now, she needed to fetch Thad his dinner—along with the bad news.

seventeen

The morning following Thad's incarceration, Susannah returned to the jail laden with creature comforts. If he had to be in this disgusting place, at least she could make his stay a little more tolerable.

Yesterday afternoon when she told him what the bank manager said, Thad confirmed Fergus McDougal's claim, admitting he had completely forgotten the nearly depleted condition of his expense account.

Unwilling to accept the ridiculous situation, Susannah had voiced the obvious. "Surely if you wrote to your father or the Union Railway Company they would send you more money. . . ."

But Thad shook his head, withering her hope. "Even if I sent a letter today, it would be at least a week—maybe two—before any money could arrive. With no way to get a telegraph to Indianapolis, I'll just have to wait it out," he'd told her.

His admission had filled her with guilt, knowing that if he hadn't given her the money for her inn payment, he could have used it for bail.

If Ruben and Lilly had just not taken that money. . . The useless thought caused Susannah's welcoming smile to quaver as she neared Thad's cell.

"Breakfast smells wonderful." Smiling broadly, he rose from a little three-legged stool, the only seat in the tiny cell.

As she stepped to the iron bars, Susannah set down the linen-covered basket filled with buttered bread, jam, sausage, scrambled eggs, and milk to better grip the clean bedding she carried in her other arm.

Sheriff Lykins murmured a polite greeting and opened the cell door, the hinges protesting with a loud squeak. Mutely, he transferred the basket of breakfast, clean sheets, and feather pillow to Thad's side of the bars.

From behind Sheriff Lykins, Susannah eyed the straw tick on the floor with disdain. "I'm sure accommodations here can't be comfortable, but maybe these will help."

"It's not the Killion House Inn by a long shot," Thad said with a little laugh, "but it's better than the bedroll I slept on many nights during my army days." His gaze held hers in a sweet embrace. "Thank you, Susannah. These will help considerably."

"I'm just so sorry this has happened to you." Susannah's anger and embarrassment about the false witness borne against Thad hadn't diminished. It hurt her to think of him caged like an animal for something he didn't do.

"Ezekiel Murdoch visited me yesterday after supper. He reminded me that all things work together for the good." Smiling, Thad lifted his Bible, which Susannah had brought yesterday at his request. "God has a reason for this, Susannah. We just don't know what it is yet."

Susannah marveled at his faith. Thad Sutton had helped her to see, acknowledge, and appreciate God's answered prayers. The flood that receded before damaging the inn, Georgiana's recovery, and Thad's advance on his rent providing her with last month's payment on her inn—she could see God's hand working in those blessings. But what good could be accomplished by his being in jail?

Her gaze swept his cramped confines. "I'm sorry Thad, but I can't see any good from your being in this dingy little cell."

"I can," he whispered. Taking her hands into his and giving them a warm squeeze, he brought her gaze back to his. "If this hadn't happened, I doubt I would have had an opportunity to spend nearly as much time alone with you these past two days."

Sheriff Lykins cleared his throat as if to remind them of his presence. Sounding embarrassed, he apologetically clicked the cell door shut. "You can use my desk chair to sit and visit if you'd like," he told her.

The back legs of the chair rasped on the bare floor as he dragged it across the room and set it near the bars. After locking the cell door, he mumbled something about an errand that needed his attention and slipped out the jailhouse door.

After asking a blessing for the food, Thad fixed Susannah with a worried frown. "Has that Macklin man bothered you. . . or been by the inn?"

Susannah shook her head and assured him she hadn't seen Mick since they saw him together at the post office. Only then did the tense lines in Thad's face relax a bit, and he dug into the basket of breakfast.

When he finished his meal, Thad set the basket aside and picked up the Bible. Thumbing through the pages, he stopped and began reading from the book of Acts, the account of Paul and Silas in prison.

"See," he said as he closed the book on his lap, "blessings can even come from being in jail." He reached his hands invitingly through the bars.

Susannah grasped his waiting hands and luxuriated in the wonderful warm tingles pulsing through her at his touch. She followed his example as he bowed his head in prayer. Hot tears pressed against her closed eyelids when Thad asked God to protect her, Georgiana, and Naomi and to give him patience and teach him what he needed to learn from this experience.

Susannah's heart throbbed with love for this man. Thoughts of what a life spent with Thad Sutton might be like teased the edges of her mind. She swatted them away. That could never be. Surely after this unpleasant experience, he would be eager to leave this place and never return.

❧

For the next three days, Susannah divided her time between the inn and the jail. The times spent with Thad in conversation, Bible reading, and prayer were the sweetest of her days. As they shared stories from their childhoods and fond remembrances of George, Susannah felt the bond between her and Thad strengthen. Although she longed for his release, a part of her knew she'd miss these visits.

The Sunday following Thad's arrest, Susannah's heart throbbed with a familiar ache as she nestled a chicken pie in a linen-lined basket for his noon meal. Although the circuit judge arrived yesterday to hear the case, nothing had changed. The judge's sentence of forty dollars or forty days brought Thad no closer to freedom. Hopefully, the posts would run smoothly and he would soon receive a reply from the railroad board along with a promissory note in the amount of his fine.

As she covered the pie with a cloth, Susannah shoved aside the painful thought that when Thad secured his freedom, he would most likely leave Promise for good.

"Is Tad coming home today?" Georgiana tugged on Susannah's skirt and asked the same question she'd asked several times a day since Thad's arrest.

Helping her four-year-old daughter understand why her hero had been put in jail presented Susannah with a formidable task. The explanation Georgiana seemed to grasp best was simply that Thad was being punished for something he didn't do.

"Not unless the railroad sends him money to pay his fine," she said and saw her own feelings reflected in her daughter's pout. "Or if we could somehow come up with enough money to pay it."

"Tad could come home if we gave the sheriff money?" Georgiana's eyes widened in her upturned face.

"Yes," Susannah said, tucking a jar of sweet tea into the basket. "It's called a fine. But we don't have any extra money."

"Dolly has money."

Susannah couldn't help grinning at Georgiana's comment. She was glad that imagination still softened the hard realities of life for her little girl.

She brushed silky curls from Georgiana's forehead and gentled her voice. "Not the kind of money Miss Lacy uses, honey. Real money, like the money guests pay to stay here."

"Not Miss Lacy. Dolly. Dolly has real money. It's in her casket." Georgiana dragged out the puzzling words in a frustrated tone.

Susannah blew out an impatient sigh. She was already late taking Thad his dinner. "What on earth are you talking about, Georgiana?"

Georgiana grasped her hand. "Come on, I'll show you!"

Reluctantly, Susannah surrendered to her daughter's tugs, leading her out of the inn's kitchen and toward the garden.

"There, by the orange flowers." Georgiana pointed to the edge of the garden where Susannah had planted marigolds to help keep insects away from the vegetables. "That's where I buried Dolly in her casket, 'cause I—we—respect her."

Susannah caught her breath, afraid to believe the notion forming in her mind. Could it be? Could the cash box she'd thought stolen by Ruben and Lilly actually be lying buried here beside the garden? Dropping to her knees, she grasped her daughter by the shoulders. "Georgiana, did Lilly get the casket for Dolly?"

Georgiana shook her head. "Lilly just brought the pieces of Dolly to the garden. Then Ruben came and said they needed to go and they left. That's when I got the box. Thad said that we bury people in caskets to show re–respect. So I had to find a casket to bury Dolly in."

"Where, Georgiana? Where did you get Dolly's casket?" Susannah's heart pounded, praying Georgiana's answer was what she suspected.

"In the step. It's the box you keep in the step." She hung her little head and a tremor ran through her tiny voice. "Am I going to be punished?"

Susannah's heart melted at her daughter's tears. She understood that Georgiana's actions had been prompted by a sincere wish to honor her destroyed plaything. "Do you know what you did was wrong?"

Georgiana nodded.

"Do you promise to never take anything again without asking me or Grandma?"

Giving another nod, Georgiana sniffed and wiped her hand under her nose.

Susannah kissed her daughter's tear-dampened cheek. By admitting she'd taken the cash box, Georgiana had shown true courage in her desire to help Thad. "No, honey, you will not be punished."

Turning her attention to the mound, Susannah began frantically digging in the soft dirt with her bare hands. Her fingernails soon scraped against something hard. As she brushed dirt away from the object, she immediately recognized the oak cash box. Holding her breath, she exhumed the little casket from its shallow grave.

She lifted the hinged lid, conflicting emotions surging through her, then released her breath in a relieved puff of air at what she saw. "Oh, thank You, God," she whispered.

On a bed of bank notes, the pitiful broken pieces of Georgiana's beloved Dolly lay scattered among a dozen or so gold and silver dollars.

Guilt diluted Susannah's joy. She would need to write Ruben and Lilly, telling them of her suspicion and begging their forgiveness.

She looked at Georgiana's sad little face, and her heart constricted. Although it had been necessary, she'd disturbed Dolly's resting place. Taking her child's hand in hers, she looked Georgiana in the eye. "I will find another casket—a better one—for Dolly. And this time I will help you have a proper funeral for her. We will even sing some hymns."

Georgiana ran the back of her hand across her wet cheek and nodded her agreement.

Rising, Susannah swiped at the dirt clinging to the front of her skirt. "But first, we need to get this money to Sheriff Lykins so Thad can come home."

Home. How wonderful if that were really true. Susannah's heart twisted, knowing Thad Sutton would never be making a permanent home here in Promise.

❧

"Did you kill me to have my wife?"

Shaken, Thad sat up in bed. Breathing hard, he ran a trembling hand over his sweat-drenched face. Many times since the war, he'd been awakened by dreams of long-past battles. But this had been far more personal. The accusing specter of George Killion had seemed so real.

Since his release from jail yesterday afternoon, Thad had wrestled with the question of asking Susannah to be his wife. When she'd burst into the jail with the cash box and the fantastic story about Georgiana having buried it, she'd swept all doubt from his mind and heart. No other woman on earth would do for him.

Yet the old question that had tortured him since his arrival in Promise last April slinked again from the darkest depths of his conscience. Deep in his heart, he knew he had chosen to stay in Promise at the Killion House Inn while working on this stretch of the surveying job because of Susannah. Had he come here to meet and woo the widow of the man he sent to die? And what if he did? And what if by some miracle Susannah agreed to be his wife? Would he see George's accusing image gazing at him in the shaving mirror every morning for the rest of his life?

Thad knew that Susannah would always own his heart. Nothing would change that. But did his love for her make him a latter-day King David? The thought sickened him.

Throwing back the covers, he slipped from the bed and crossed the dark room on unsteady limbs. The pale glow of the moon shafting through the open window cast eerie shadows on his bedroom wall. They did nothing to dispel the dream-induced apparitions that had tormented his sleep.

The pitcher shook slightly as he lifted it from the washstand and poured some of its contents into the bowl. He splashed the tepid water on his face, allowing it to trickle down the front of his nightshirt.

He walked to the window where cool evening breezes fanned the wetness on his face, sending a shiver through him. Below, the canal—a silver slash in the moonlight—dissected Promise. Three months ago when he arrived from Cincinnati via the hapless ditch, he would never have imagined the effect it would have on his life. The good people of Promise despised him as if he'd come to assassinate a beloved family member. But oddly, the thing that had made Thad a pariah in Promise—the canal—had inextricably twined his life with Susannah Killion's.

And beyond his own concerns about his feelings for Susannah, there was the matter of his father's letter, which had arrived yesterday demanding that he return to Indianapolis. There had been no mention of Thad's request for money. The two letters undoubtedly passed in the mail. The words of his obviously irate parent had branded themselves upon his brain.

. . . .You will, and without hesitation, return to Indianapolis, forgetting this Killion woman and that mud hole with the ironic name, Promise. You should know that as of this date, your Union Railway expense account has been closed at Promise Bank. Also, you have been invited to the governor's ball to be held the evening of Saturday, July five, which I expect you to attend. There, you will ask the lovely Miss Olivia Vanderpohl to become your bride. Any deviation from my orders will result in your immediate dismissal from the employ of the Union Railway Company. . . .

Thad trudged back to the bed, sinking with an agonized groan to the feather mattress. If he defied his father's orders, he would lose his job as well as his father's esteem. But if he did as Josiah Sutton demanded, he would lose all hope of having the woman he loved. Either way, Promise, the Killion House Inn, and Thad's hope for a happy life all seemed doomed.

eighteen

"He will be back, daughter."

Susannah stopped folding napkins on the dining room table and jerked at Naomi's soft words and gentle touch on her shoulder. She turned away so the older woman would not see the renegade tear that had escaped the corner of her left eye.

"I doubt it," she murmured, not even attempting to pretend she didn't know who Naomi meant. She seemed able to read Susannah's mind. Although often irksome, that insightful quality in her mother-in-law felt oddly comforting to Susannah at this moment.

It had been more than a week since Thad Sutton simply disappeared from Promise. Yet his leaving without a word still stung. The only hint of where he'd gone had been the letter she'd found beneath the writing desk in his room. She felt a little guilty about having read a missive not intended for her eyes, and now wished she'd dropped it, unread, into the lost-and-found bin behind the front desk. Obviously, he had bowed to Josiah Sutton's demands. In a few short days, Thad would be promised to Olivia Vanderpohl.

Susannah plopped a neatly folded linen napkin atop a pile of a dozen others and strove to affect a cool, detached tone. "It just seemed a cruel thing to do to Georgiana." Careful to keep her back to Naomi, she walked to the buffet and deposited the napkins in the top drawer.

Naomi smiled from the stove where she poured hot water from a whistling teakettle into a stoneware pitcher. "That's why I know he'll be back. Captain Sutton loves that child." She sent Susannah a knowing look. "And you know as well as I do,

Georgiana is not the only person in Promise he holds dear."

Susannah's heart echoed Naomi's claim, and she wanted to believe them both. But Naomi had no knowledge of the letter. And even if Thad did love her, it didn't change the fact that his life belonged in Indianapolis with the Union Railway Company and Olivia Vanderpohl. Besides, as shabbily as he'd been treated in Promise, she couldn't really blame him for leaving after he'd been freed from jail.

Naomi hefted the steaming pitcher and headed toward the door to the hallway. Pausing at the threshold, she looked over her shoulder at Susannah. "I'll get Georgiana ready for the church's Independence Day picnic right after I take this shaving water to the drummer in room 204." She gave a little laugh. "That man is a true salesman. He even tried to sell *me* a plow."

"Thanks, Naomi." Susannah smiled as love and gratitude for her mother-in-law swept through her. What on earth would she do without Naomi? Susannah also appreciated the fact that Naomi had made no fuss or fanfare when she began joining her again each morning for scripture reading and prayer. She might not always agree with Naomi, but Susannah thanked God daily for George's mother.

"Are you sure you don't want to take Georgiana to the picnic? I'd be glad to stay and watch the inn." The kindness in Naomi's faded blue eyes caused tears to sting at the back of Susannah's.

"No, you and Georgiana go on." She grinned. "I don't mind missing a few patriotic speeches, and with everyone at the celebration, it will give me a good chance to catch up on bookwork and to inventory the supply room." Susannah's answer had been honest, but the real truth was that she had no heart for any sort of celebration.

A half hour after Naomi and Georgiana left for the church, Susannah sat behind the big oak desk staring unseeingly at her ledger book. The figures in the columns blurred, replaced by the image of Thad standing at the front of a church with Olivia Vanderpohl.

Susannah's heart constricted painfully, and a tear trickled down her cheek. She swiped at it impatiently. *And that is exactly where he belongs.*

She needed to forget Thad Sutton—forget how they'd worked side by side to save the inn from the flood, forget the time they'd spent together in Bible reading and prayer, forget the tender moments they'd shared in the blackberry thicket, forget the feel of his arms holding her as they prayed for Georgiana's recovery. And mostly, she needed to forget the sweet touch of his lips on hers.

Two large teardrops splat onto the ledger page, smudging the carefully inked figures. Sniffing, she wiped the back of her hand across her wet cheeks. Yes, the sooner she forgot Thad Sutton, the better. She must focus on her job—keeping this inn going. And that task had become all the more difficult in light of the coming railroad.

"Susannah."

Susannah's head jerked up at the masculine voice. Half expecting to see the man who'd dominated her thoughts, she blinked surprised into Garrett Heywood's face. Since it was Friday, she hadn't expected to see him until tomorrow.

"Didn't mean to startle you." He twisted his blue wool cap, his gaze not quite meeting hers. "I have a favor to ask of ya."

What kind of favor could Garrett mean? "You know you can rent a room on credit if you need to. . . ."

"It ain't that." He pushed his fingers through his russet hair as his brown-eyed gaze settled at last on her face. "It has to do with Sallie."

"Is Sallie all right?" Susannah had wondered if there was a problem with the *Flying Eagle* when Garrett and his boat hadn't appeared in Promise last Saturday. Maybe Sallie had been sick, but surely he'd have simply found another cook until she recovered.

"Sallie's well." He cleared his throat loudly. "Thing is"—his gaze went skittering about the lobby again—"Sallie wonders if you might take her on here. You know, like you did Mick Macklin's girl."

His request puzzled Susannah all the more, causing her to blurt out the question that sprang into her mind. "Did you give her the sack?" she asked in a surprised whisper. Susannah couldn't imagine Garrett being so cruel to his longtime cook. And even if he had ended her employment on his canal boat, why would he be trying to find her another position?

Garrett's normally ruddy face deepened to an even redder hue, and he shook his head. "No, I didn't give her the sack. We kinda come to this decision together in Cincinnati." He cleared his throat again. "Sallie and me, well, we come to an understandin'."

"Understanding?" Perhaps Sallie had just decided she didn't want to work on a canal boat any longer. "What kind of understanding?" Susannah just wished Garrett would stop beating about the bush and say what he meant.

"Me and Sallie have an understandin' between us. But bein' Christian people, we don't reckon it'd be seemly to keep spendin' so much time together on the *Flying Eagle*. I suggested we just get hitched in Cincinnati, but she's got her heart set on a proper church weddin' here in Promise and—"

"Wedding? You and Sallie?" Susannah stared at Garrett and felt her jaw go slack. Since Sallie was such a devout Christian, Susannah had never imagined linking the two romantically. But now that she thought about it, since the church social in April Garrett had attended every church service when he'd been in Promise on the Lord's Day. Susannah knew Garrett must have sincerely turned his life around or Sallie would never have agreed to such a match, even if she was in love with him.

He gave her a sheepish grin. "Funny how a man can't always see that what he really wants has been in front of him all along." His gaze dropped to his hands wringing the wool hat.

Unable to suppress a wide grin, Susannah rounded the desk to give him a quick hug. "Oh Garrett, I'm so happy for both of you!"

And she was.

Susannah sent up a silent prayer of thanks that God had not allowed her to become so lonely she succumbed to the charming canal captain's past overtures. Her friend, Garrett, would have a wife who truly loved him, not one who felt she merely settled for a convenient husband.

"It would only be until after the weddin'," Garrett said. "Sallie wasn't comfortable askin', seein' as how you and me had sorta..."

Sensing his unease at the awkward situation, Susannah rushed to Garrett's assistance. "Of course she can stay here. Though I can't pay her much, Naomi and I would be more than grateful for the extra help."

Garrett blew out a long breath and the tense lines in his face relaxed. "No pay is necessary. I'll see to it that Sallie has everything she needs." His brown eyes fairly danced, and an ever-widening smile marched across his broad, ruddy face. "Me an' Sallie appreciate it, Susannah."

After repeated thanks, Garrett left the inn, promising to return later with his intended.

Several minutes later, pencil and paper in hand, Susannah entered the storeroom. An annex of the kitchen, the storeroom jutted out from the inn's main structure between the kitchen and dining room. The earthy aromas of coffee, molasses, root vegetables, and flour assailed her nostrils as she made her way through the hodgepodge of crates, sacks, and kegs.

She couldn't help smiling again at Garrett's news and looked forward to Sallie's stay at the inn, however brief. Perhaps she and Naomi could even help the future Mrs. Heywood in planning her and Garrett's wedding.

A twinge of envy squiggled through Susannah. She couldn't help thinking that if not for the railroad and Olivia Vanderpohl, she, too, might have been offered a marriage proposal.

In her heart, Susannah knew Naomi was right. Thad Sutton had cared for her—maybe even loved her. But obviously not enough to defy his father.

Blinking back hot tears, Susannah tried to erase the image of Thad and Olivia from her mind by focusing on the work at hand. But after counting the kegs of molasses twice, she still had no idea what number to write on the scrap of paper.

Tucking the pencil behind her ear, she sank wearily to the top of a wooden crate and gazed at nothing.

And what if he had asked me to marry him? Would I have accepted?

The question she had avoided for months now demanded an answer.

No.

No. Even though she loved him, Susannah knew in her heart she would've declined an offer of marriage from Thad Sutton.

Why?

She knew the answer.

George.

Clearer than it had been for months, George's smiling face came into sharp focus before her mind's eye. Susannah knew that even if it hadn't been for the railroad or Olivia Vanderpohl, George's memory would not have allowed her to accept a future with Thad, or anyone else for that matter.

George was with God. Her heart was finally at peace with that. So why couldn't she let go?

Fear.

Here in the quiet of the storeroom, Susannah at last came face-to-face with the truth.

She couldn't remember when she hadn't known George. George was safe. George was familiar. Theirs had been a relationship formed in childhood and, in a way, it never really matured. Since his death, she'd hidden behind George's memory, using it as an excuse to not subject her heart to the uncertainties of grown-up relationships.

Until Thad.

Despite her best efforts to keep it locked tight, Thad had opened her heart and allowed her to glimpse the hope of a future beyond widowhood.

Tears streamed down her face unheeded. Perhaps that was God's reason for sending Thad to Promise—to teach her heart it was capable of loving again.

Her gaze flitted toward the sound of a faint squeak. Sitting quietly, she watched a gray mouse appear from behind a molasses keg. Its tiny pink nose constantly twitched as it nibbled on a grain of corn. When the corn had been consumed, it sniffed the floor around the area where the corn had been. Seemingly satisfied that no other grains of corn remained, it scurried away behind the kegs. Even a mouse had sense enough to know when it was time to move on.

Susannah knew at last she was ready to move on, too. Ready to do the thing she had so long resisted. Ready to put the past behind her. All she needed was the courage to grasp whatever future God had in store for her.

The scripture verse from Psalm 31 that Naomi read before breakfast this morning sprang to Susannah's mind.

"Be of good courage, and he shall strengthen your heart, all ye that hope in the LORD."

Dropping to her knees, Susannah clasped her hands in prayer. "Dear Lord, help me know how to move on. I never want to forget George, but for Georgiana's sake as well as my own, give me the courage to live whatever life You have planned for me."

The image of a yellowed envelope floated behind her closed eyelids—the letter Thad had brought with him to Promise. By refusing to read George's last letter, she'd attempted to keep her marriage to George alive. She knew now it had been God's voice talking to her heart each time she'd felt a nagging tug to open the letter. Even though she had turned away from God, He had never left her. She'd just been too stubborn and angry to follow His direction.

Snuffling, she dried her eyes on her dress sleeve. "Thank You, Lord." She grasped the rough wooden lid of the crate in front of her and rose, knowing that she'd never be able to go on with her life until she'd read that letter.

"Ah, there ya be."

Susannah whirled at the slurred voice behind her.

A leering grin stretched across Mick Macklin's scraggly bearded face. He took a couple of unsteady steps toward her, bringing with him an overwhelming odor of stale sweat and whiskey.

"Don't seem to be anybody else in the place." Laughing, he gestured with upraised hands. "Maybe now that we're alone, you might be more in the notion to tell me where my girl is." His grin vanished and his eyes narrowed to cruel slits.

Susannah's mind raced as she fought the fear threatening to paralyze her. Normally she wouldn't have concerned herself with the drunken buffoon. But here, in the confined space of the dim storeroom, he presented a real menace.

Slowly stepping backward, she tried to assess her best hope of escape. She knew the door to the outside was locked. Her only way out of the storeroom was through the door that led to the kitchen, and Macklin had that route blocked.

Continuing to put more distance between them, she hoped to lure him farther into the room, distracting him with conversation. Then maybe she could slip past him back into the kitchen.

Though her throat had gone sawdust-dry, Susannah forced a calm tone to her voice. "I will tell you that Lilly is safe. Beyond that, I think it's up to Lilly to let you know of her exact situation."

"Ya do, do ya?" His mouth twisted in an angry snarl as he advanced.

With a quick glance to her right, Susannah mentally mapped her escape route. *Around the potato bin, along the inside wall, and then follow the shelves holding the canned goods to the door that leads to the kitchen.*

She took another step backward and felt the calf of her right leg smack against something solid. Thrown off balance, she fell backward onto what she realized must be a pile of flour-filled sacks.

"Ahhh!" She scrambled to right herself, but Macklin had reached her.

Grasping her shoulders, he pushed her harder against the flour sacks. "Mayhap if we was to get a little more friendly like, you'd be more willin' to tell me what ya know about Lilly."

Raw terror grabbed at Susannah's insides. *God, help me! Please, help me!* She beat her fists against his disgusting bulk while rolling her head away from his yellow-toothed sneer and rancid breath.

Suddenly, she remembered that Garrett would be bringing Sallie back to the inn. *Dear Lord, please let them be in the inn!* Gasping for breath, she screamed as loudly as Macklin's bulk pressing on her chest allowed. "Garrett, help me! I'm in the storeroom! Please, help me!"

With eyes closed, she continued to beat futilely at Macklin until suddenly his weight lifted off her and she was beating at thin air. Opening her eyes, she gaped in disbelief as Thad's fist cracked against her assailant's jaw.

nineteen

Susannah shivered in the July heat, still marveling over her miraculous deliverance. The events of the past half hour played over in her mind, keeping her emotions and her stomach churning. While Thad guarded her subdued attacker, she'd hailed a passing reveler and asked the man to summon the sheriff. Then when the lawman arrived, she spent several uncomfortable minutes relaying to him Macklin's drunken attack on her.

From her seat on the bench beneath the oak tree, she expelled a ragged breath as she watched Sheriff Lykins shake Thad's hand before marching Mick Macklin away in handcuffs. With the ugly incident finally behind her, she sent up a bevy of thankful prayers.

"Are you sure you're all right?" Joining her on the bench, Thad took her trembling hands into his.

"Yes, just a little shaken up." Susannah forced a smile she couldn't quite hold steady. "I never imagined you'd be back—I mean—leaving in the night the way you did."

A penitent look clouded Thad's gray eyes before his gaze dropped from her face to their clasped hands. "I'm sorry," he murmured. "I know I should have said something." He lifted his face again, his gaze seeming to beseech hers for understanding. "But I had pressing business that required my attention in Indianapolis, and I didn't want to wake you or Georgiana."

Susannah couldn't help wondering if Olivia Vanderpohl constituted pressing business. She drew her hand from his. "You could have left a note. . .so Georgiana wouldn't fret."

A pained look crossed his face. "Did she fret?"

Susannah slowly shook her head. She almost wished she could say yes and punish him for sneaking off in the night. "No, she's gotten used to you leaving Promise and then later coming back. She just assumed you'd come back."

"But you didn't." There was no hint of a question in his voice.

"No."

The word hung in the air between them as they sat listening to the pop of distant firecrackers and faint shouts of "Huzza!"

" 'And a little child shall lead them.'" A smile traipsed across his face, setting Susannah's heart throbbing painfully.

Why does he have to be so handsome? Why does he have to be so good?

To hide the tears springing to her eyes, Susannah turned away, looking down the canal at a boat decked out in patriotic bunting. Somehow—she didn't know how—she must make her heart give up Thad Sutton. Whatever plans God had for her life, they couldn't include him. If not already promised, he would soon be affianced to Olivia Vanderpohl.

When she trusted her voice again, Susannah forced a light tone. "So, did you conclude your business?"

Grinning, he reached into his coat pocket and withdrew a folded paper. "Actually, yes." He held the paper toward her.

Puzzled, Susannah accepted the unexpected offering, unable to guess what it might be. Unfolding it did little to clear her confusion. It simply looked to be some sort of legal document peppered with lawyer jargon such as "whereas" and "wherefore."

"It's an agreement signed by every member of the railroad board to situate a depot in Promise when tracks along this stretch of the railroad are laid," Thad said in answer to her quizzical glance. "I, along with my father, successfully convinced the board that situating a depot in Promise would be a prudent decision."

Remembering Josiah Sutton's tone in the letter she'd read

and his disdain for Promise, Susannah's confusion mounted. "But he said in the letter—" she blurted and then gasped, realizing her mistake.

It was Thad's turn to look surprised.

Unwilling to meet his gaze, Susannah stared unseeingly at the legal document in her hands. She hated having to admit her lapse in etiquette but knew she must explain her comment. "I—I found your father's letter in your room. I know I shouldn't have read it, and I sincerely apologize for doing so."

"Ah, I see." His quiet voice did nothing to douse the shame burning inside her. He cleared his throat. "When I returned to Indianapolis, I confronted my father concerning his demands, and we had a—discussion."

The pause before the word suggested to Susannah that it must have been a heated discussion.

His voice lowered. "We finally spoke plainly, man-to-man, as we should have done a long time ago."

"But your father seemed so—insistent." Susannah couldn't help believing there must have been more to it than simply Thad's powers of persuasion.

He fidgeted on the bench and rubbed his palms down the tops of his thighs, his gaze seeming to study the post office porch several yards beyond the National Road. "I let him know in no uncertain terms that I would not be bullied or blackmailed. I'm not especially proud of the fact, but I threatened to destroy the work I'd done unless the board agreed to my terms—a passenger depot in Promise."

Gratitude balled up inside Susannah. Thad had actually gone to battle for her inn. For Promise. She wondered at what cost. "Was your father angry?"

Thad shot her a grin. "Oh, yes, very angry. But I think he actually respected me for the first time in my life. I was as surprised as anyone when he joined those voting in favor of placing a depot here."

"And Mr. Vanderpohl?" she asked in a near whisper, worried

that Thad was now on unfavorable terms with his future father-in-law.

Surprisingly, Thad gave a soft laugh. "Old Vanderpohl was beside himself. I thought he might have a conniption fit right there in the boardroom. In fact, he gave me the sack."

Susannah emitted a soft gasp. Hot tears sprang to her eyes as regret twisted her heart. Thad had sacrificed his position—not only with the railroad, but with his father—for her. "But—but surely Miss Vanderpohl could intercede on your behalf...."

Thad took Susannah's hands, folding his fingers warmly around hers. "I did not see Olivia, nor do I have any desire to see her, Susannah."

The soft, almost whispered tone of his voice sped Susannah's heart to a gallop. Holding her breath, she met his gaze and studied the serious intensity drawn on his face.

A quick twitch, like a wince, drew down his brows for an instant. "Susannah, I've been doing a lot of praying and soul-searching. That was another reason I needed to get away from Promise. Away from your nearness."

His throat moved as he paused to swallow. His gray gaze looked deeply into her eyes as if attempting to see all the way to the center of her heart. "I love you, Susannah. I love you more than I ever imagined I could love someone. But, because of George, I had to be sure that none of my past actions were dishonorable, which would taint the affection I have for you."

With his thumbs, he caressed the backs of her fingers while he blew out a long breath. "After much reflection, my heart is at peace and I am sure. And so, Susannah Killion, I ask you now...will you do me the honor of becoming my wife?"

During Thad's rambling and rather convoluted proposal, Susannah sat gaping at him, all at once astounded, mystified, and giddy. She'd barely recovered from the shock of his return to Promise. And now, he'd set her heart and head spinning again with a marriage proposal she could never have seen coming.

Having no idea what to make of his obscure references to

soul-searching and dishonorable past actions, she fought the urge to laugh. Would she never get a normal proposal from a man?

George's best effort had simply been to say, "Well, Susannah, we're eighteen, so I reckon it's high time we got married."

Though she longed to say yes to Thad, Susannah knew she couldn't—not yet. Not until she'd read George's letter and put that part of her life to rest.

She gave his fingers a gentle squeeze and looked deeply into his hopeful eyes. "Thad, I care for you very much. But I cannot give you an answer just yet. There is something I need to do first. May I give you my answer tomorrow?"

A pained look flitted briefly across his face, but his quick, warm smile dispelled it. "Yes, of course. I understand. Take what time you need."

The sound of rockets exploding in the distance echoed the fireworks igniting inside Susannah. Though her every impulse clamored against her restraints, urging her to accept his offer without hesitation, she knew it would not be fair to Thad for her to leap into a future with him—this marvelous future God had opened up to her—until she'd closed the book on her marriage to George.

But her eager heart ached for the morrow.

❧

It was long past dark when an excited Georgiana finally drifted off to sleep. All afternoon the child had danced and whooped at the return of her hero. Susannah's heart had joined in Georgiana's glee when Thad presented the little girl with a new china doll tea set he'd brought from Indianapolis.

Smiling, Susannah bent and brushed a golden curl from her daughter's brow, now serene in sleep. How happy Georgiana would be to learn that the man she adored would soon be her new father.

The night breeze fluttered the lacy curtains framing the open window. An occasional faint *hiss* and *pop* bore evidence to the continued Independence Day celebrations.

Susannah opened the top drawer of her dresser, her heart ready for its own emancipation from the past. She lifted out George's letter, sat on the edge of her bed, and broke the envelope's wax seal. In the sputtering candlelight, she began reading the left-slanted script of her late husband.

Dear Susannah,

It's comin' on to twilight now, and though there's a little chill in the air, it's right warm for February. We're holed up here in a mountain pass called Buena Vista. Santa Anna thinks he's got us on the run, but old General Taylor has other plans. He figures the Indiana Second and us in the Third, along with some Illinois boys and Jeff Davis's Mississippi Rifles, can give the old Mexican a run for his money.

Going to be a battle tomorrow for sure and it's shaping up to be a real ripsnorter. Captain Sutton, he don't feel right comfortable about our situation. That's the reason I'm writing this. He's asked me to head up a scouting mission soon as it gets dark to learn how close the Mexican line is to our flank. The Mexicans know this country, and finding them in the dark without them finding us could be a real trick. With you and our baby weighing heavy on my mind, I asked Captain if I might pass on this one. But he allows I'm his best tracker and the only man he trusts to head up this mission. Captain Sutton's a good man and I trust his judgment. But if you're reading this, then I reckon I didn't make it back. I want you to know I love you. Always have. You're the strongest, smartest girl I ever knew, and my heart is easy, knowing you will be able to see after Ma and the inn. Tell Ma I love her, too. If the baby's a boy, I'd be right proud if you'd name him after me. If it's a girl, well, you name her what you think is best. I sure would have liked to see our baby, but I reckon I'll see you both one day in heaven.

Love,
George

The words blurred through Susannah's tears, and she wiped her drenched cheeks. Suddenly, her gaze drifted to the date of the letter—February 22, 1847—and a cold chill slithered through her. She was sure that was the date Thad had noted as George's date of death. George had said the battle was expected the next day, and she knew few battles were waged at night.

Dropping the open letter, Susannah snatched the pewter candlestick from the top of the dresser and rushed to the trunk at the foot of her bed. She sank to the floor, the skirt of her nightgown splaying around her, and opened the trunk's metal latch. As she lifted the lid, the peculiar smells of the cedar-lined trunk tickled her nostrils.

In the flickering candlelight, she rummaged beneath a pile of Georgiana's baby quilts and dresses until her fingers touched the edges of an envelope. Pulling it out, her heart cinched painfully. Thad's now-familiar bold script was scrawled across the front of the yellowed envelope. She set the candlestick on the floor and slid out the folded missive.

Perusing the page, she fought sobs as the letter unleashed the same overwhelming sense of grief and loss that had caused her to faint when it arrived four years ago. Drawing a ragged breath, she corralled her feelings and searched for the information she dreaded to confirm.

Susannah gasped as her gaze fixed on the date of her husband's death. As she read Thad's words, her heart, along with any hope of a happy future with him, shredded against the cold, jagged edge of fact.

It is my unhappy duty to inform you that your husband, George, died valiantly this day, February 22, 1847, in service to his country. May God's grace and everlasting peace. . .

Susannah dropped the letter back into the trunk. Her heart echoed the dull thud as she closed the trunk's lid. On February 22, 1847, Thad Sutton had sent George on a dangerous mission. A mission from which George had requested to be excused. The mission that cost him his life.

She sat on the floor, hugging her shaking frame until her agony solidified to a rock-hard anger. Pressing her hand against her mouth, she battled nausea as a wave of revulsion swept over her. How could she marry the man who sent George to his death?

twenty

All night Susannah tossed as sleep fled from her tortured mind and heart. Long before dawn, she surrendered any hope of rest and slipped quietly from bed. Praying Georgiana might sleep late this morning, she dressed and made her way down to the kitchen.

In the kitchen, she busied herself with her usual morning tasks, knowing this morning would be anything but usual. Thankfully, there were several guests who would need breakfast before the ten o'clock stagecoach arrived. Also, Sallie O'Donnell would have to be schooled in the care of the inn. Susannah feared none of these chores would be enough to crowd out the pain that last night's discovery had unleashed.

She opened the door to the side yard and closed her eyes as a morning breeze bathed her face. The gentle summer zephyr caressed her troubled brow with tender fingers.

Why, God? Why?

It was the only prayer her numbed mind could form.

Opening her eyes, she watched the dawn tint the canal, transforming it into a shimmering ribbon of pink. The sky had begun to lighten above the little woods. Somewhere in the distance, a rooster crowed.

She turned her gaze toward the woods, and a jumble of painful memories played before her mind's eye. She and Thad, with Georgiana on his shoulders, laughing together as they crossed the meadow, off to hunt mushrooms on a fine spring day. And then she saw the three of them wading through knee-high summer grass toward the blackberry thickets. Could she ever again look at the meadow and not see Thad's

156

stalwart figure striding through the grass with his surveyor's tripod resting on one broad shoulder? Could she ever again pick blackberries and not feel his arms holding her, his lips tenderly caressing hers?

The shrill whistle of the teakettle pierced her anguished reverie. Turning back to the stove, she swiped at her tear-washed cheeks.

The time had come. Today, Thad would be expecting her answer to his marriage proposal.

She wrapped a piece of quilted flannel around the teakettle's handle and poured the steaming water into a stoneware pitcher. Her jaw clenched with her rekindled anger. With Captain Thaddeus Sutton's shaving water in hand, she started for the stairs.

Well, now he will get his answer!

ès

Thad had just pulled on his second boot when three sharp raps sounded at his bedroom door. His heart sped to double-time cadence. This was the moment for which he'd waited through the torturously slow nighttime hours.

For the most part, sleep had eluded him. Different scenarios of why Susannah Killion might have postponed her answer to his proposal had chased endlessly around his mind.

The only viable answer had formed one name—Garrett Heywood.

Yesterday afternoon, when Thad had wandered through the inn looking for Susannah, it had been her frantic cries of Heywood's name that alerted him to the storeroom. But if she had her heart set on Heywood, why didn't she simply tell him yesterday when he proposed?

The moment he opened the door, Thad sensed something was terribly wrong. The look he saw on Susannah's features sent warning bells clanging in his brain.

No hint of a smile softened the rock-hard lines of her face, and her gaze seemed intent on evading his. "Your shaving water, Captain Sutton," she mumbled as he took the pitcher from her hands.

"Susannah, what's wrong?" The impersonal frostiness of her tone slashed at Thad's heart like icy shards. He had fought in hand-to-hand combat on the battlefield, but he'd never felt the kind of fear that twisted inside him now.

Her chin quivered as it lifted, and she met his gaze. "George didn't die in the Battle of Buena Vista, did he?"

"No, he died in a skirmish the evening before the main battle," he said. As he carried the hot water to the washstand, Thad's mind raced. Hadn't he mentioned that fact in the letter he sent her four years ago? He couldn't remember.

At the washstand, he turned to face her and was stunned by the raw anger flashing from green eyes that glistened with unshed tears.

"You sent George on a dangerous mission—a mission he didn't want to go on—and he died. Isn't that right, Captain Sutton?"

The scorn with which she enunciated Thad's name felt like a dagger through his heart. Thad could not imagine how Susannah had only now learned the particulars of her husband's death. And it didn't matter. The incident that had haunted him for four years had been dragged from the dark dungeon of his conscience into the glare of daylight. And the woman he loved had become his accuser. He swallowed painfully. "Yes," he managed in a defeated, rasped whisper.

Her whole body trembled and one lone tear breached its lovely confines to slip unhindered down her rose petal pink cheek.

Thad longed to take her in his arms. He stepped toward her, arms outstretched.

Shaking her head, she wrapped her arms around herself and took a step backward. "Don't touch me!"

Thad blew out a sigh, and his heart deflated. Somehow, he must make her see the situation that faced him that February evening in 1847.

"Susannah, please, you must understand. I was responsible for a whole company of men. I had to know just exactly where the enemy was camped. George was my best tracker."

She narrowed her eyes at him, and her words sounded tight, as if shoved through clenched teeth. "And all you cared about was winning the battle."

Thad winced at the memory of George handing him Susannah's daguerreotype and a final letter for safekeeping in the event he didn't return. She would never know that he wept that night over the loss of Sergeant George Killion.

"Susannah," he told her somberly, "because of George, the mission was a success. George didn't make it back, but the two men he led on the mission did. Their information saved our company, and perhaps a large portion of our regiment."

Susannah's stiff demeanor showed no indication of softening or any sign that his words had made an impression. Her arms seemed to tighten around her body, and her chin lifted in a stubborn tilt. "I'm afraid I cannot have you in my inn another day, Captain Sutton. Please be good enough to vacate this room before breakfast." With this chilly proclamation, she whirled from him and fled down the stairs.

The July morning sun streamed through the window, bathing the room in a golden glow. But its warmth never touched the cold debris of Thad Sutton's shattered heart.

❧

Susannah closed the pantry door after instructing Sallie O'Donnell on the different foodstuffs, their placement, and the amount of each that needed to be kept there. Earlier she'd done the same with the linen closets, shown Sallie the register and ledger books and how they should be kept, and gone over the rules having to do with the room keys, protocol concerning guests, and every other minute detail of running the inn she could think of. Anything that would take her mind off Thad.

"I'll never remember all this in one day." The look in Sallie

O'Donnell's brown eyes reminded Susannah of a doe she'd surprised once in the little woods.

Susannah's conscience stung with regret. She touched Sallie's arm. "Oh, of course I never meant for you to get it all at once. I was just trying to acquaint you with. . ."

Susannah's voice faded at the half-truth. What she was really trying to accomplish was to clutter her mind until thoughts of Thad had no chance of slipping in. So far, her attempts had failed miserably.

It hadn't helped when she'd witnessed Garrett kiss Sallie's cheek before he departed for Cincinnati on the *Flying Eagle*. Although happy for Garrett and Sallie, the joy of their newfound love seemed to underscore Susannah's pain at the loss of her own.

Naomi stepped into the kitchen from the storehouse, her apron laden with onions and carrots. "Sallie," she said, giving the woman a bright smile, "why don't you begin cleaning these. Later you can help me make a big pot of cressy soup."

The relief on Sallie's face smacked again at Susannah's conscience. It had never been her intent to overwhelm the woman.

Naomi emptied her apron of vegetables onto the worktable then turned a kind smile toward Susannah. "Come, daughter," she said while brushing her hands a couple of quick swipes down her apron. "Sallie tells me she's had her prayer and scripture reading time this morning, but I'm afraid we've been remiss in our own."

Susannah followed Naomi toward the lobby's sitting area. The knowing look on her mother-in-law's face told her the older woman had a specific subject in mind for their daily devotional. Naomi hadn't said a word to Susannah concerning Thad's hasty departure. But Susannah felt fairly certain that was about to change. She'd known Naomi Killion far too long not to realize her mother-in-law suspected there'd been a rift between her and Thad.

Naomi settled herself on the green velvet settee and patted the seat beside her, inviting Susannah to sit.

Susannah obeyed. Taking her mother-in-law's proffered hands, she closed her eyes. Other than unintelligible wailings of her heart, Susannah had not gone to God about her confrontation this morning with Thad.

Naomi's slight, work-roughened hands squeezed Susannah's. "Dear Lord, be with us this day and help us to see Your perfect will. I especially ask that You heal the contention that has come between my daughter and Captain Sutton. Salve their broken hearts and lead them in Your way of love and forgiveness."

Susannah yanked her hands from Naomi's and met the other woman's quizzical gaze. "Thad sent George on the mission that killed him, Naomi," she blurted. "George told me in the letter Thad brought last April." Shame dragged down her voice. "The letter I finally read last night."

Naomi cocked her head, a sad smile softening the deep lines of her face. "Susannah, George was a soldier, and Captain Sutton was his commanding officer. When Captain Sutton spoke to me of George, I could tell that he carries the burden of George's death with him still."

An incredulous breath puffed from Susannah's lips. "How can you defend Thad Sutton when he ordered George to his death?"

Naomi reached for Susannah's hands again and sighed. "Daughter, I am defending no one. Like you, when I learned my boy had been killed, it left a George-shaped hole in my heart. I knew I couldn't bear to live that way, so I asked God to fill it with love and forgiveness, and He did. I forgave the Mexican soldier who killed our George. I must also forgive Captain Sutton for any order that might have put George in the way of that Mexican soldier."

She paused as if considering her next words. "I don't think you ever asked God to help you forgive, Susannah, and I wonder if your anger at Captain Sutton has something to do with the argument you and George had before he left."

Susannah winced as her mother-in-law's gentle chide touched a raw nerve. What good did it do to remind her of past offenses? And what did it have to do with how she felt about Thad?

Naomi turned her attention to the Bible on her lap. Seeming to thumb purposefully through the whispering pages, she paused at last and began to read from the second chapter of Second Corinthians. " 'So that contrariwise ye ought rather to forgive him, and comfort him, lest perhaps such a one should be swallowed up with overmuch sorrow. Wherefore I beseech you that ye would confirm your love toward him.' "

The words convicted Susannah. During the past several months, she'd come to know Thad's heart. Despite her accusations this morning, she knew he was anything but uncaring. In her heart of hearts, she knew George's loss would have grieved him. Had her own pain and need to blame someone for George's death caused her to heap undeserved sorrow upon Thad?

Naomi moved her finger slowly down the page and continued reading. " 'To whom ye forgive any thing, I forgive also: for if I forgave any thing, to whom I forgave it, for your sakes forgave I it in the person of Christ.' "

She looked up from the book and fixed Susannah with an intense gaze. "Susannah, you love Thad. But this is tearing you up inside. It's just like when you found out he was surveying for the railroad. But in time, you came to care about him, so you looked past that. Unless you can find a way to forgive Thad, you will never have peace about this."

Susannah knew Naomi was right, but the wound on her heart from what she'd learned from George's letter was still too fresh. And somehow, her anger toward Thad felt like a shield. *Against what?*

"Mamma, Gwamma!" Georgiana came bounding into the sitting area, Miss Lacy tucked under one arm and her eyes grown wide. "It's really windy outside, and it's raining ice balls!" She opened her fist to display a dirty ice nugget melting across her grimy palm.

At Georgiana's announcement, Susannah stopped to focus on the sound of hail pinging against the inn's roof.

Susannah and Naomi turned in near unison toward the long, narrow window just beyond the lobby. Leaves ripped from their branches whipped past in an atmosphere colored a sickly green.

Naomi's face went ashen and she sprang from the settee. "Susannah, we need to get everyone to the storeroom. Now! I'm afraid a cyclone may be coming!"

twenty-one

Thad leaned forward in the saddle and pulled his hat brim down lower on his face to fend off the wind and rain as his horse plodded along the muddy road. In the two hours since he'd left Promise, the weather, along with his mood, had markedly deteriorated.

Still numb from Susannah's rejection, he tried to focus on the sixty-mile journey before him. But he couldn't erase from his mind the hurt and anger he'd seen in her eyes. How she learned the details of Buena Vista remained a riddle. But he didn't blame her for her angry reaction. How could he expect her to forgive his decision when he hadn't been able to fully forgive himself for making it? He also knew that at some point, he would've had to tell her anyway.

He gripped the saddle's wet leather pommel until his hand hurt. *I should have told her. I should have told her right off before I let myself. . .*

A sardonic chuckle burst from his lips. Before he what? Before he fell in love with her? He knew that had been a *fait accompli* within the first twenty-four hours after he'd arrived in Promise.

The wind gusts had grown stiffer, driving the rain like wet needles against his face. Chieftain jerked his head up and down, neighing and snorting in protest at the inclement weather to which he was being subjected.

Squinting, Thad peered through the near deluge. He would need to avail himself of the next structure that offered shelter for him and his steed. It was bad enough being miserable on the inside. No sense in remaining miserable on the outside as well.

As he rounded a bend in the road, the brackish-gray form of a hip-roofed barn came into view. Riding up to it, he saw that one of the barn doors had been left open. He guided Chieftain into the shelter, praying the farmer wouldn't appear and shoot him for trespassing.

The familiar barn smells of hay, wet straw, leather, and manure welcomed Thad to the rustic haven. Two milk cows mooed in their stalls at the intrusion, while a team of mules looked up from munching hay with only mild interest showing in their dark eyes.

Thad dismounted, tied Chieftain to a slat in one of the stall gates, and lowered himself to a somewhat clean-looking pile of straw. With his back against a rough-hewn support post, he blew out a long, weary sigh.

Gazing out at the rain-soaked vista beyond the open barn doors, he suddenly felt tired. So very, very tired. His lack of sleep last night, coupled with Susannah's scathing rejection this morning, had drained his energy. The soft, pattering sound of the rain on the barn roof seemed to drag down his eyelids.

Oh, Lord, if she can never love me, please, just let her not hate me. The agonized prayer was his last conscious thought before sleep overtook him.

A sharp, jabbing pain in his side caused Thad to jerk awake, blinking.

Above him, a large, full-bearded face scowled down from beneath a black slouch hat. Thad was glad to notice that at least the pitchfork in the farmer's hands was turned handle-down. He realized the blunt end of the tool handle must have inflicted the pain near his midsection.

Thad scrambled to his feet. "I'm sorry, sir. My intentions were not to trespass but only to seek shelter for me and my horse." He glanced toward Chieftain happily sharing hay with the two mules.

The big man raked a slow, suspicious look down Thad.

At length, a satisfied smile lit his face like the sun that now streamed through the open barn door. He held out a beefy hand. "You're more than welcome, stranger. Thought mayhap you were a drunk or a bummer." The scowl returned for an instant. "Cain't abide drunks and bummers."

Thad accepted the farmer's firm handshake then brushed straw from his shirt and pants, hoping the man wouldn't change his opinion. "No, sir. I'm on my way to Indianapolis. Just came from Promise."

The farmer gave a long, slow whistle. "Reckon you're in the Good Lord's debt then." He cocked his head toward the opening in the barn. "A feller came by 'bout an hour ago and said a cyclone hit Promise. Flattened half the place and near emptied the canal."

The blood drained to Thad's toes. Dread gripped his insides at the thought of a cyclone tearing apart the Killion House Inn. Visions too awful to contemplate swam before his mind's eye. Had the inn been hit? Was Susannah all right? He had to know. "Were—were there any injuries?"

The farmer's shoulders lifted in a quick shrug. "Feller didn't say. Cain't imagine there wouldn'ta been though."

With an unsteady hand, Thad rummaged in his trousers pocket, brought out a couple of coins, and offered them to the farmer. "Thanks for the shelter," he mumbled, untying Chieftain.

The farmer accepted the coins, dragged off his hat, and scratched grimy fingers across his balding head. "Don't need to rush off. The wife's likely made plenty o' dinner. You're more'n welcome to stay."

Mounting Chieftain, Thad shook his head and wheeled the horse toward the open barn door. "Thanks for the invitation, but I have to go."

"Never get to Indianapolis tonight," the farmer hollered from inside the barn. "So where you headed in such an all-fired hurry?"

"Promise," Thad called back, praying God had seen fit to spare the Killion House Inn and the lives of those dear to him.

&

"Mamma, Miss Lacy don't like the dark."

At the whimper in Georgiana's small voice, Susannah hugged her child tighter, rocking her on her lap. Only precious, narrow shafts of light and air filtered down through cracks around the edges of the root cellar's ill-fitting trapdoor. Susannah was proud of how well her little daughter was handling the frightening, unexpected confinement. Neither did Susannah like the dark, dank hole that crawled with myriad insects and smelled of musty earth and rotting root vegetables. She forced a light tone to her voice. "I know, darling, and we'll be getting out soon."

Susannah prayed she was right. How long had it been since the seven of them sought shelter beneath the storeroom's floor—an hour, two hours? She found it impossible to judge. An interminable amount of time seemed to have passed since she and Georgiana, along with Naomi, Sallie, and the inn's three guests clambered down the short ladder to take refuge in the six-by-eight-feet cellar.

Moments after Susannah pulled the trapdoor over them, the most menacing roar she'd ever heard filtered into their little hidey-hole, making her ears pop. Clinging to Georgiana, she'd joined Naomi and Sallie in prayers for deliverance, though their words were swallowed in the din of the tumult.

After several terrifying minutes, the unearthly wailing and crashing sounds had abated, leaving only an eerie silence that felt worse than the cyclone's noise.

Eager to emerge from the dark, cramped space, Susannah had hurried to the ladder beneath the cellar's trapdoor. Standing on the third rung, she'd reached up and pushed against the little square door, but to no avail. Something seemed to be blocking their only escape route. Their refuge had become their prison.

The two men among the group, a young newlywed with his

equally young bride and the dapper-dressed plow salesman, tried numerous times, without success, to free the group from their little dungeon.

But now, as the minutes dragged by, a general feeling of frustration had given way to a sense of unease that Susannah feared bordered on panic. Sallie clung to Naomi and muttered snatches of broken prayers while the young bride wept softly against her husband's shoulder.

The black-mustached farm equipment salesman, who seemed to have run out of stories to tell, became increasingly more fidgety. "Let me take another whack at that door," he said, making his way around the young couple huddled against the wall.

Susannah scrunched nearer Naomi to give the man room. Trying to ignore the strong smell of sweat and bay rum fanned by the drummer's movements, she prayed for his success.

After several fruitless shoves and a few mumbled words that caused Susannah to clamp her hands over Georgiana's ears, the drummer managed only to shower them with bits of loose dirt. Muttering his apologies, he returned in defeat to his previous spot behind the newlyweds.

Susannah watched the young couple embrace, the husband comforting his fretful wife. Suddenly, visions of Thad holding her and comforting her flashed before Susannah's mind's eye.

The words from the scripture Naomi had read this morning echoed hollowly inside Susannah. *"Lest perhaps such a one should be swallowed up with overmuch sorrow."* She remembered how she'd sent him away—swallowed up with sorrow—into the jaws of the storm. She'd sent him off in anger. *Just as she'd done to George!*

Now she understood what Naomi had meant when she'd said Susannah's anger at Thad had something to do with her argument with George all those years ago. Susannah realized she'd never forgiven herself for not making up with George before he left for the war. That was what she'd never faced. It had always been easier to be angry with someone else. First with God, and then with Thad.

Guilt, remorse, and an unfathomable sadness swirled inside Susannah like the cyclone they'd come down here to escape.

The cyclone!

Thad was out there, somewhere in the open, at the mercy of the storm. At the mercy of the cyclone. Fear grabbed Susannah's belly in an agonizing grip.

Oh, dear Lord, I did it again. I sent someone I love off in anger to die! Dear Father, please let him be all right. Please. . .

In the dim light, Naomi's gaze caught Susannah's, fixing on her tear-drenched cheeks. A calm smile graced Naomi's lips. She reached over and caught Susannah's hand, giving it a quick squeeze. Then she turned to Sallie, who'd been softly singing hymns. "Wonderful idea, Sallie. Why don't you lead us all in song? It will lift our spirits and maybe someone will hear us."

For the next several minutes, Sallie and Naomi led them all in choruses of "Rock of Ages" and "Oh God, Our Help in Ages Past."

As the women began the first verse of "My Faith Looks Up to Thee," the words convicted Susannah's heart.

> *My faith looks up to Thee,*
> *Thou Lamb of Calvary,*
> *Savior divine!*
> *Now hear me while I pray,*
> *take all my guilt away,*
> *O let me from this day*
> *be wholly Thine.*

Susannah knew she would never be right with God until she asked Him to take away the guilt she still carried from her trespasses against the two men she loved. *Oh, Lord, do take away my guilt so I can be wholly Yours.*

Remembering the loving words of George's last letter, Susannah felt sure that her husband had, indeed, forgiven her for her anger at his departure. Now, with God's help, she would strive to forgive herself. The moment she emerged from this cellar, she would write to Thad and beg his forgiveness for her callous treatment of him this morning. She needed him to know that she no longer held George's death against him.

Her continued thoughts of Thad made him so real to Susannah that she imagined she heard his voice calling her name.

"Susannah? Susannah, are you here?"

The sound became clearer, convincing Susannah it was not her imagination. Her heart thumped so hard she gasped for breath.

"Stop. Stop!" she called, breaking into the song's chorus and even dousing the drummer's hearty tenor. She sprang to the ladder, climbed to the second rung, and pounded on the trapdoor. "We're here! We're down here!"

"Are you all right?" Thad's anxious voice, muted by the barriers between them, drifted down into their dark confines.

"Tad! It's Tad!" A gleeful Georgiana began hopping up and down, clapping her little hands.

"Yes, we're all right." By force of will, Susannah reined in the urge to follow Georgiana's example. "Please, get us out."

"Thank You, Jesus!" The words came out in a whoosh of his breath. "There's a tree limb blocking the door," he called down after a moment's pause. "I'll need to find something to use as a lever to get it off."

Susannah's own prayer of thanks lifted from her grateful heart. *Yes, thank You, Jesus! Thank You that he's here and unhurt!*

She wondered how much damage had been done to the inn. But knowing Thad was here and that he was safe negated all other concerns.

After several more minutes of scraping and grunting sounds, the trapdoor popped open.

The relief Susannah felt at the rush of light and fresh air into the stifling cellar was almost overwhelming. She immediately lifted Georgiana up to Thad's waiting hands.

Susannah's heart swelled when Georgiana, still clutching Miss Lacy, hugged Thad's neck and said, "I'm glad the storm didn't get you, Tad."

"Me, too, moppet," Thad said with a chuckle as he lowered her to the storeroom floor.

The guests were next to exit the root cellar, followed by Naomi and Sallie who voiced their hearty thanks to God and His servant, Thad Sutton.

At last, Thad reached down and grasped Susannah's hand, helping her up to the storeroom. Just to be near him and feel his hand in hers made the sight of the huge oak limb sprawled across the demolished room unimportant.

An awkward moment ensued until Thad broke the uneasy silence. "I heard about the cyclone. . . . I was afraid. . ." His throat moved with a swallow, and he glanced around the room at the destruction. He turned back to her, his voice brightening. "The rest of the inn seems sound though," he said as they watched the others head for the kitchen, Naomi and Sallie taking charge of Georgiana.

Susannah only nodded, a knot of emotion choking off any answer. What could she say knowing he'd come back to check on their safety after she'd ordered him from the inn?

Love, gratitude, and shame bubbled up inside her until, with a sob, it all broke free. The floodgates opened and a deluge of pent-up tears spilled down her cheeks. "I'm sorry. I'm just so sorry. Please forgive me. I don't blame you for George's death. You have to know I don't blame you," she said between sobs as he engulfed her in his arms.

"Shh, it's all right, my sweet. It's all right, my love. There's nothing to forgive," he murmured, rocking her in his arms and muffling her sobs against his shoulder. "It's I who should be begging your forgiveness."

She pushed away and blinked back tears that blurred his dear face. "I think all that's left for us to do now is to forgive ourselves, and with God's help, I know we can."

He answered with a slow smile that crept across his handsome face. Further conversation was postponed as he gently nudged her head back with his chin and his lips sweetly caressed hers.

"I thought you were going to Indianapolis," she whispered at last, reveling in the feel of his warm breath against her neck.

"I don't have a job there anymore, remember?" he said, nuzzling his face against her hair.

"You think you can find one here?" Susannah teased, her heart singing as she gazed into his adoring eyes.

"I thought maybe I'd try my hand at innkeeping," he said with a grin.

Susannah stifled a giggle. Another odd proposal, but it was good enough for her. New tears sprang to her eyes, misting his features.

"Yes, I think maybe you should," she whispered before he silenced her with more kisses.

epilogue

A golden shaft of sunlight slanted through the church's long, narrow window. It glanced across the strong, square jaw of Susannah Sutton's new husband, mildly surprising her.

She hadn't been aware of the moment when the rain stopped drumming on the church's roof or when the distant thunder had quieted its rumblings. She and Thad seemed wrapped in their own special sphere, apart from all happenings beyond their exclusive realm.

Gazing into his soft gray eyes, she had just now echoed the vows he had pledged to her moments before.

"You may kiss your bride," Pastor Murdoch told Thad.

A grin quirked the corner of Thad's mouth.

The instant before she closed her eyes to accept his kiss, Susannah caught a glimpse of the dimple she loved so much.

As his lips touched hers, the notion became real to her that she would actually be spending the rest of her life with this wonderful man. The thought sent a happy tear sliding from the corner of her left eye to her ear. Paradoxically, Susannah wished this kiss would never end yet at the same time was eager for her and Thad's new life to begin.

The church erupted in applause, and a giggling Georgiana bounced and clapped beside them.

Still wrapped in each other's arms, Susannah and Thad grinned down at their daughter's antics.

Swaying from side to side in her skirt of ivory lace over satin that replicated her mother's own wedding dress, Georgiana looked like a little lacy, tolling bell.

A beaming Josiah Sutton, who'd acted as his son's best man, clapped Thad on the back and kissed Susannah warmly on the cheek. Now his son's staunchest ally, Josiah had leveraged his influence with the Union Railway Company. His efforts had resulted in Thad being reinstated as the company's chief engineer and surveyor for the Cincinnati to Indianapolis project.

Through misty eyes, Susannah glanced at the front row pew. Sallie Heywood, clinging to her husband's arm, dabbed at her wet eyes with a linen kerchief. Susannah had been happy to learn that Garrett and Sallie would soon be selling the *Flying Eagle* and opening a dry-goods store in Promise.

Shifting her gaze to her mother-in-law's face, Susannah returned Naomi's pleased smile. She'd read Naomi's mind too many years not to decipher the sentiments glistening from her brimming blue eyes.

Susannah gave her mother-in-law a nod of agreement. She, too, was sure that from somewhere in heaven, George was smiling down upon this happy moment.

Thad scooped up Georgiana then wrapped his other arm firmly around Susannah's waist. Together the new little family headed down the aisle and out the church's double doors.

There they paused, and Susannah caught her breath at the remarkable vista before them. A vivid rainbow arched across the slate gray sky.

"Look, a rainbow!" Georgiana pointed at the colorful scene from her perch on Thad's arm.

Susannah breathed in the fresh, rainwashed air, struck by the sense that for her, Thad, and Georgiana, God had made the world anew. The symbol seemed so personal, as if the Lord were reminding her to never again doubt His promises. And she knew she never would.

"Yes, my darling," Susannah said, leaning her head against her husband's shoulder, "it's the symbol of God's promise— His everlasting promise."

A Letter To Our Readers

Dear Reader:

In order that we might better contribute to your reading enjoyment, we would appreciate your taking a few minutes to respond to the following questions. We welcome your comments and read each form and letter we receive. When completed, please return to the following:

Fiction Editor
Heartsong Presents
PO Box 719
Uhrichsville, Ohio 44683

Did you enjoy reading *Everlasting Promise* by Ramona K. Cecil?
❏ Very much! I would like to see more books by this author!
❏ Moderately. I would have enjoyed it more if

_____
_____
_____

Are you a member of **Heartsong Presents**? ❏ Yes ❏ No
If no, where did you purchase this book? _____
_____

How would you rate, on a scale from 1 (poor) to 5 (superior), the cover design? _____

On a scale from 1 (poor) to 10 (superior), please rate the following elements.

_____ Heroine   _____ Plot
_____ Hero   _____ Inspirational theme
_____ Setting   _____ Secondary characters

5. These characters were special because? _____

_____

_____

6. How has this book inspired your life? _____

_____

_____

7. What settings would you like to see covered in future
   Heartsong Presents books? _____

_____

_____

8. What are some inspirational themes you would like to see
   treated in future books? _____

_____

_____

9. Would you be interested in reading other **Heartsong
   Presents** titles? ❏ Yes ❏ No

10. Please check your age range:
    ❏ Under 18   ❏ 18-24
    ❏ 25-34   ❏ 35-45
    ❏ 46-55   ❏ Over 55

Name_____

Occupation _____

Address _____

City, State, Zip_____